RAIDER'S SKY

RAIDER'S SKY

A NOVEL BY MARY HAYNES

Lothrop, Lee & Shepard Books
New York

First Edition 1 2 3 4 5 6 7 8 9 10

Library of Congress Cataloging in Publication Data
Haynes, Mary.   Raider's sky.
Summary: After a chemical accident kills off most of the world's population, twelve-year-old Pokey escapes from the regimentation of the Children's Concern and finds a new life and hope for the future with a group of elderly people living in West Virginia.
[1. Science fiction]   I. Title.   PZ7.H3149148Rai   1987   [Fic]   85-23788
ISBN 0-688-06455-8

NOTE: Places, signs, and street names do not necessarily correspond to those in the real Harpers Ferry.

To G. Lee and Judy

Contents

RAIDER'S SKY

PROLOGUE
Catastrophe

IT WASN'T SUPPOSED TO HAPPEN. No one had anticipated such an event, imagined or prepared for it.

At one P.M. on a late spring day, a strange green cloud drifted up from a field in north central Nebraska. The cloud was a by-product of a simple agricultural experiment, a combining of chemicals to make a strong fertilizer. Unexpectedly, impossibly, the new compound fed on air and multiplied, growing and moving in every direction.

By four o'clock eastern time, the cloud covered most of America. In Arlington, Virginia, near Washington, D.C., ten-year-old Pokey Hughes was on the swings behind her apartment building with her baby brother, Jimmy. She heard sirens and, looking around, saw the air change color. Clutching Jimmy, she fled upstairs, screaming for her mother.

Mrs. Hughes was chopping onions. She dropped her knife, hurried with Pokey to the big double bed, and pulled the covers over all their heads. Jimmy squawked. Pokey held her mother's hand, afraid to speak. When she peeked out, the green mist was in the room, staining the air.

1

* * *

Two days later, Congressman John McQuarter attended a top-secret briefing for government officials. A four-star general spoke. "I'm sorry, gentlemen and ladies. We're in big trouble. The cloud, it seems, was an accident. Nothing nuclear, nothing we'd *been* worrying about. But . . . poison."

John McQuarter put his head in his hands. *No,* he thought. *No, no, no.*

Ross Jacobson was fourteen years old. He was in traction, in a hospital in Denver, with a broken leg. He had been dozing when the mist came, then watched in horror as the news was broadcast on the TV above his bed. The cloud had gone all the way around the world, touching every bit of air before it vanished.

The TV's stopped; nurses didn't come. A new disease was killing staff, patients, countless newcomers. The telephone by Ross's bed worked sporadically, but late one night he got through to his home. "Sorry, boy," the caretaker told him. "Your parents are dead." Ross wept and raged at the ceiling, lay still for long hours, sure the disease would take him as well.

The third day, confused but healthy, weak only from hunger, he climbed out of traction before he starved to death.

There were hundreds of sick people in the hospital, crowding the halls, coughing, weeping, staring. Silent. The symptoms became well known: a green rim in the whites of the eyes, heavy bones, swollen glands, hard breathing. An attack on the body's systems from within.

Ross scooted around in a wheelchair, doing his best to help, keeping busy so he wouldn't have time to think.

* * *

Six months later, at the start of the first winter, an old woman named Hannah Lucas walked along the cold banks of the Shenandoah River near Harpers Ferry. *Seems I'm not going to die*, she thought. *Oh, Lord, give us strength.*

When the worst was over, one out of every thousand or so people survived. Although their bodies had absorbed the poison, they were unaffected, immune, like some people who never get chicken pox. *One* out of every thousand. Oddly, most of them were children.

Faced with such devastation, society splintered back into something like wilderness. Nothing worked. Telephone circuits couldn't take the overload; they fizzled, and shorted out for good. No one manned the power plants, stood before TV cameras, put together *Time* or *Newsweek*, delivered the mail. Some individuals talked to each other on shortwave radio, but this communication only made clear how much had been lost.

In the countryside, lone survivors coped primitively, almost as pioneers had before the age of electricity. In old cities, strangers drifted together to form new groups, helping one another. There was little contact between regions; life was too hard.

Washington, D.C., became the seat of one such tiny government. There, most people stayed in their desolate dwellings, too sad and lost to come out. But others, finding solace in work, got busy.

"We have to haul away the dead," they said. "Bury or cremate them.

"Generate electrical power. Get some kind of news service going. Get in touch with stranded people.

"The water seems all right. But didn't the poison touch everything? Better be careful what we eat!

3

"Children—all these leftover children. We'll have to take care of them."

Emerging leaders formed into teams called the Food Concern and the Children's Concern. More came (former government officials, electronic wizards, store clerks), and they created a central headquarters in the old Position Room of the State Department. The group wasn't large—never more than a hundred members—but they worked long hours, using the city's old know-how to solve new problems.

A local TV system was set up, and messages from headquarters began probing in a seventy-mile radius (to Baltimore in the north, around to the Appalachian foothills, down into Virginia, and back up the Chesapeake Bay). The broadcasts were intended to soothe people and give instructions. Every day, listeners were told what to do, what to avoid, and how to obtain a little safe food.

The Children's Concern began rounding up unclaimed children to care for them centrally. Astonished at how many young people they found, the CCers wondered, "Why were *they* immune? Doesn't seem fair." The kids were unhappy, in a kind of survivor's shock that didn't end, and their keepers kept that state of shock current: "Makes handling them so much easier. And it's only temporary."

Rarely (once in eight, then twelve, then twenty weeks) a curious, heroic pilot would roar over the city and land his plane at National Airport. From Dallas, London, and Tehran, these men brought tales of slow rebuilding elsewhere. They came seeking supplies or help, but always had to leave empty-handed. The visitors frightened everyone. Isolation was preferable, safer.

Time passed. Twelve months after the cloud, it was

4

spring again, and vegetables that had rotted on vines the year before seeded themselves and started to grow. Members of the Food Concern announced: "Don't eat anything fresh! Earth and seeds might hold concentrations of the Green Mist poison. Swallowing such elements could retrigger illness."

That summer, new strains of old diseases, such as dysentery and cholera, raged through the city. People were dying once more, from the flu.

The following winter was hard, surprisingly gray and more gray.

As the second spring approached, the now-established leaders grew worried. Nothing was back to normal. Most of the population still huddled in their apartments, depressed and useless. The children were becoming a burden. Washington's small stores of food, produced and packaged before the disaster, dwindled alarmingly. Summer was coming, with hot weather health problems bound to recur.

The old capitol was no longer the leader of anything; trouble seemed just beyond every curve.

CHAPTER ONE
Second Spring

"POKEY, WAKE UP. IT'S GETTING LATE."

"Wha . . ." Pokey opened an eye. It was Trudy speaking, from the next cot. "Oh, hi, Trudy. Wait a minute."

Groaning as she turned over, Pokey wiggled her toes, unable to just leap out of bed. She closed her eyes, listening to the sounds of movement around her, wishing she were somewhere besides the big Internal Revenue Service building in Washington, D.C., where she lived in a dim corridor with fifty-three other twelve-year-old girls.

She'd been here for over a year, and still couldn't get used to morning.

It was two years since the green cloud had come and everything changed. But even now, sometimes in her sleep she forgot (not that she dreamed; her sleep was thick and dark, like pudding) and woke thinking, *What?* Then lay immobilized as memory came flooding back. If the others had such moments, they never mentioned them. Pokey didn't either, exactly. But she was often in trouble for saying too much.

"Clean clothes today." Trudy was sitting cross-legged, examining between her toes and rubbing them clean. She didn't look up.

Pokey mumbled, "Unhh," got her dirty clothes from the wire basket under her cot, and padded over to the supply area near the elevators. She dropped her bundle in the big USED LINEN cart, then walked along the bins and pulled out what she needed: some navy shorts marked GIRLS TRACK, crew socks, a once-pink sweatshirt, and dingy, over-bleached cotton briefs. She thought longingly of her own underwear. BLOOMIES, they'd said on the bottom, with purple polka dots. Pushing the thought away, she went back to her bed to get dressed.

Before she was done, up and down the hall above their heads the TV's whined and came to life, showing Matron Celeste Shrank's smiling face, with her sharp nose and square chin.

"Good morning. Everybody up?" She couldn't see them, of course, and didn't wait for answers. The girls sat on their bunks or stood where they were, staring at the screen.

The TV's had only one channel, bringing Matron from her office downstairs or the bland announcer from central headquarters. Many times a day the sets would flicker and spout long streams of announcements and instructions. No entertainment, music, or stories. That was past.

Matron Shrank continued. "It's a lovely spring morning. Dress accordingly. Some people will get outside today." Pokey touched her bare legs. *Glad I picked out shorts,* she thought.

Matron swung right into the words she said every morning, a soothing litany: "Remember. We have lived through a terrible time. We have survived but the aftermath is bad. The Children's Concern is taking care of things. We take care of the worry. We are not afraid. Remember, until we are strong we cannot be normal. There is solace in work. We will take care of you."

7

She looked down, her image holding every upturned face. "Now repeat with me: Remember. We are safe here. All things are temporary. They will take care of us. Remember we are safe here. Safe.

"Repeat." They did.

"And again." Pokey said the words with everyone else, believing them.

Or almost believing them.

She told herself every morning, *You aren't any more wounded than anyone else. You can forget. You don't have to ask questions and be troublesome.*

She thought of all the grown-ups (in the Children's Concern, the Food Concern) who worked so hard. And the many hundreds of children stacked up in government buildings. Everyone else seemed to know how to behave. Pokey vowed to do better.

Matron Shrank said brightly, "Now, today's work assignments." She read down the list of corridors and duties until she came to Pokey's section. "IRS—Fifth floor, twelve-year-old girls. Report to Kitchen One. Peel potatoes."

"Ugh." Pokey made a face. "Not again."

Trudy smiled. "It's better than the days we sit and do nothing."

"Just barely."

At the end, Matron said, "One special announcement. We will be taking some children away this morning, on a little trip." The picture faded. "Brush your teeth."

Pokey pulled at the covers, slapdash making the bed, then shuffled her straight brown hair with her fingers as she moved along in line with the others, up the stairs to the cafeteria on the seventh floor.

Matron Shrank herself was there, tall and broad, holding a clipboard. "Ah, Pokey." She made a mark on her list and pointed toward the auditorium. "You go there."

With a small wave, Trudy had already vanished. Pokey looked where Matron was pointing. Miss Vanderpugh, another of the hard-working grown-ups, had come out of the auditorium and was hurrying toward them. Pokey couldn't help smiling.

"Hi," she blurted. Miss Vanderpugh was her favorite and Pokey was glad to see her.

The woman didn't acknowledge Pokey's greeting, but said to Matron, "Oh, no. Not this one, too?"

"Yes, of course." Matron held up the list. "Portia Elaine Hughes. That's you, isn't it, Pokey?"

Pokey nodded. No one called her Portia except on official occasions, and she wondered, *What's going on?*

Miss Vanderpugh protested, "But—"

"We have a duty, Miss Vanderpugh. And a quota."

"But—"

"Come now. Summer's near. You'll not balk at *this* one?" Matron Shrank whispered but Pokey's hearing was excellent. " . . . a perfect choice: always lagging behind, asking questions. She can use a rest."

Boys and girls of all ages, from all floors, crowded into the hall behind them. Pokey was a bottleneck.

Matron nodded and, tight-lipped, Miss Vanderpugh led the way into the auditorium and left Pokey with a cluster of children.

Questions crowded Pokey's mind. *What was that about? Why is Miss V. upset? Should I trust Matron Shrank. Do I? She scares me.*

More children came. Gradually, they moved closer together, almost touching, sharing wordless sympathy as they always did when frightened or faced with change. Pokey unfocused her eyes and repeated the litany, *Remember. We are safe here. All things are temporary . . .* until

9

Miss Vanderpugh returned and announced, "Breakfast."

They filed into the empty cafeteria, ate thick gray cereal, and waited.

"Well, here we are. Good, good." Matron clapped her hands in the doorway. "Let's go now, lucky ones."

"Lucky?" Pokey asked, her voice louder than she'd intended.

"Yes." Matron smiled, her glance flicking over the group. "You're going on a journey."

"Where?" asked a boy named Martin, touching Pokey's sleeve as if for courage.

The smile seemed to glaze. "Ohio State."

Pokey frowned. Many children (mostly over the age of fourteen or fifteen) had been taken to work on experimental farms. But others had disappeared as well; she never heard where they went. Had they gone to Ohio, too?

Closing ranks, the group marched down the hall, down the seven flights of stairs, footsteps ringing, with Matron at the head of the line, Miss Vanderpugh at the rear. They filed out of the building, into the quiet of Washington, D.C., straight up the middle of Tenth Street.

Pokey hadn't been so far away from the IRS building for a long time. Crossing Pennsylvania Avenue she saw people walking in the distance. Her group turned right and passed open-doored, plundered stores and businesses. In a high window she saw a woman watching them, and wondered how they looked: a line of sixty or eighty kids, marching two by two, the sun shining down on them. The woman waved and Pokey paused, about to wave back, when someone behind her said, "Hey, keep moving, whatcha doing?"

They walked all the way to Union Station. (Pokey remembered with a lurch in her stomach: *Oh. We met my grandmother here once. Met her train* . . . And forced the memory away.) The station was empty, echoing, until deep inside they found a large waiting room and another group of children. A man and woman stood with them, wearing sturdy white jumpsuits and worried expressions.

Pokey hesitated. "Who are they?" she asked a boy with too-big glasses perched crookedly on his nose.

"Leaders of the CC," the boy whispered. He and Pokey stopped, and the line moved around them like water flowing around a rock.

"The Children's Concern," she quoted automatically, " 'is taking care of things. We take care of the worry,' but . . . do you know where we're going?"

He squinted and shrugged. "No."

"Ohio," she told him. "That's far away."

"Yoo-hoo," Matron Shrank called. "Here we are. All accounted for."

"Yes, good. Ah, Matron," the woman began. "Tom and I—"

The man interrupted. "You'll have to wait here for a while. We're going to pick up some more equipment."

"Why?"

"It's a perfect day. When we stop for the naming, Helene and I will make a film. For television. To show why we're moving all these children around. . . ."

He smiled and Helene finished for him. "Might as well prepare explanations. Avoid trouble. OK?" They didn't wait for an answer. They left.

Matron Shrank opened her mouth, blinked, and closed it. Then she turned her back and stood by a glass door marked TO THE TRAINS, tapping her foot, stiff and mute

Miss Vanderpugh circulated. "Sh-h-h. Sit down."

11

Pokey followed. This one grown-up had always been a friend. "What's happening?"

Miss Vanderpugh frowned, twisting some of her reddish hair into the bun on top of her head. "Happening? Why?"

"Why are we going to Ohio?"

"I . . ." she began. "It's only temporary. You know that. There are . . . so many children—" She rubbed her hands nervously. "If we can get things running smoothly, without so many . . . *bodies* to care for, then we'll bring you back. That's the plan."

She looked upset, brushing at her face, her mouth clamped tight. "I . . . they . . . just leave me alone, OK?" she whispered.

"Sure."

Unsettled, Pokey circled the room, once, twice. Then lowered herself to the concrete floor. Wrapping her arms around her knees, she put her head to one side and let everything drift by, unfocused. It was the kind of fog she knew how to float in for a long time.

After several hours, the engineer came from the train, scratched his head when told no one knew how much longer they would have to wait, and led Miss Vanderpugh to an old storage room in the basement. She came back with peanut butter and cheese cracker packets and cans of warm soda. "They've been boxed and wrapped all this time," she said. "Should be safe to eat." The crackers were very stale but no one complained. After a while she collected the empty wrappers and cans. And the waiting resumed.

Suddenly Tom and Helene were back, stirring the air with motion. "Here we are. Sorry it took so long."

Pokey blinked and yawned. She was stiff from sitting.

Matron snapped, "It's three twelve. You've been gone

12

all day." No one ever worried about exactly what time it was. That, too, was past. So Pokey knew, *Matron's mad.*

"Yes. Well." The man shrugged. He was laden down with equipment. "We're ready now."

Miss Vanderpugh stepped in front of him. "Wait a minute. I've been thinking. Why don't we stop this?"

"What?" Helene demanded.

Pokey kept her head down, pretending to be asleep.

"This whole project. So far away," Miss Vanderpugh's voice quavered. "It's a mistake. Wrong."

"Now, see here." Matron sounded disgusted.

Tom talked fast. "We're lucky to have Ohio State. You know that. All self-contained. Facilities there, labs—"

He sounds like a salesman, Pokey thought. *Don't know why Miss V.'s so upset. I like to travel.*

"Willing workers," Tom continued. "You think they'd help us in Harrisburg? Ha! It's lucky I knew about Ohio. My brother—"

"Yes, yes," said Matron as if she'd heard it all a hundred times.

Helene interrupted coldly. "This isn't our first trip. You were outvoted weeks ago, Miss Vanderpugh. If you can't handle it, you should change jobs, work in the kitchens."

"No, no. I—"

"It's hard on all of us." Helene gestured broadly. "Load the kids. And spruce them up, Matron, can you?" She swept through the glass doors.

Miss Vanderpugh bent to wake a sleeping four-year-old, and Matron called, "Line up."

The girl in the next seat kept her eyes on her folded hands. Pokey turned to the window, curious, as the city slipped away. In the countryside she saw a few people, who watched the train as if standing at attention; two cows, and a big brown dog.

When they'd been under way for nearly an hour, Matron counted everyone, then walked up and down the aisle, fixing them up. She combed Pokey's hair and rubbed her face with a damp, sour-smelling cloth. The train roared past a faded sign announcing Brunswick, then through the town itself; flew along a river, into a tunnel and, blasting its whistle, clattered across a bridge, screeched, and stopped.

"All right, everybody." Matron closed the door to the car ahead and stood facing them. "Up now. Getting off."

Pokey remembered her geography. "This isn't Ohio."

"Of course not." Matron glared at her, irritated. "We make one stop along the way. This one."

A tall boy with sparse blond hair pointed out the window. "That's a river. I . . . used to live by a river."

There were several small gasps. No one ever spoke of where they had lived or what had happened. Such talk was not only painful, it was forbidden.

Matron's voice was hypnotic. "Yes, Andrew. Remember. We have lived through a terrible time." She was saying the litany. "We have survived but the aftermath is bad. The Children's Concern . . ." Her tone was low and commanding and, finally, soothing.

When she came to the children's part, Pokey moved her mouth without saying the words, watching Andrew. He didn't speak at all but stared at the window.

Matron saw him, too. She repeated gently, "Andrew, remember. We are safe here . . . Andrew?" He looked up and finally did whisper the words.

Pokey looked at her feet; she had been holding her breath.

There was an awkward silence until Matron Shrank

14

clapped her hands and said, "Well. Here we are. We're getting off. First you will be photographed and named. For the record. Then we are going on a nice tour of Harpers Ferry, and our friends Tom and Helene from the Children's Concern will make a videotape of you, for all the people in Washington to see."

She held up a hand. "Make me proud! Don't straggle, don't gawk. Breathe through your nose! Come now, one by one."

The line crept forward. It was late afternoon. Out the window, Pokey noticed a small stationhouse, and a man in overalls and a striped cap talking to Tom and Helene. Surrounding the station was a parking lot crammed with abandoned cars. When she reached the door Pokey saw why the line moved so slowly: a TV camera mounted on the underside of the station roof was photographing each of the children in turn.

"Right here," Matron motioned. "Stand in the circle."

It was a big white O painted on the sidewalk. Pokey stepped inside. A loud clicking sound came from somewhere above her. "What's that noise?" she asked.

"The electronic files at headquarters. Quick now, you're dawdling. Look at the camera." Pokey looked up; red lights flickered and Matron intoned, "Portia Elaine Hughes. Also known as Pokey."

Pokey tried to smile. "That's me."

The files clattered louder, then *click-click-clickety-click!* they stopped, and a man's voice said, "Got it. Next?"

"Next!" Matron called. "Step lively."

Pokey joined the others, standing near the edge of the parking lot.

After all three carloads of children had been processed, Tom and Helene walked up and down the row, examining them.

"Too many," announced Helene. Tom agreed, and they sent the nearer half back to the train. Pokey remained in the tour group, standing on one foot, then the other. Sometimes she thought waiting would drive her crazy.

"Ready." Tom held the microphone, with sound recording equipment slung around his neck.

Helene adjusted the camera. "Right. Let's get started. Mr. Clinton!"

"Yes, yes, here I am." The heavyset, red-faced man in overalls hurried out from the stationhouse. He walked to the front of the line, bobbed his head at the camerawoman, and gave a quick swipe to his mouth.

"I'm Skip Clinton. Stationmaster here and caretaker of this town and all its . . ." He searched for the word.

"Environs," Matron Shrank prompted.

He blinked at her. "Right. And all its parts. This town is Harpers Ferry, West Virginia. It used to be a National Historical Park, because of John Brown's raid and all the things that happened here. I keep it up real good. Just in case . . . anybody wants to come back." He grinned. "Or visit. Like you. Follow me, I'll show you."

They followed, like a lumbering, jerky toy on a string, threading among the empty cars in the parking lot to a short driveway that led down to the street.

"Stop!" cried Helene. "This is a great shot. Start talking, Clinton."

"But . . . there isn't much interesting, right here."

"It doesn't matter. Go on."

"Oh. OK. These . . ." He gestured before him. "These are the backs of houses." He started telling about how old the town was, and the hard times it had seen. Pokey didn't listen. The houses held her. Each one had a large white X painted beside the door.

16

"The X's," she murmured, feeling dizzy. She couldn't take her eyes off them, couldn't stop remembering.

After the sickness ebbed, sometime during the long months when all was confusion, work crews came to her old neighborhood in Jeeps, with canvas-covered dump trucks chugging along behind. They were searching for fire hazards, broken gas or water lines. And hauling away the dead. . . .

She had forgotten where she was. She said aloud, "One man . . ."

"Sh-h!" Tom hissed. He covered the microphone with his hand. "We're recording."

One man had come to her apartment. He knocked first, then walked in. Pokey was hiding in a wicker trunk near the door to the balcony. She glimpsed his face— he was crying—and heard him moving through the rooms. He saw no one. He marked her door with a big white X and went on to the next apartment. The team stayed on her street for two days while she watched, unseen, from her windows. The dump trucks were filled and filled and filled again. . . .

Miss Vanderpugh was standing beside her. Pokey hugged her arms to her chest, elbows to her sides. "I . . . remember."

"Of course you do," Miss Vanderpugh whispered. "But please be quiet."

Skip Clinton continued. "Now if you'll just come this way—" He led them down the driveway, along a pot-holed lane, up an alley to Main Street.

17

"The town is built steep, as you can see. Right around us is the oldest part, it's like a museum, what used to be the Historical Park. On up the hill is residential. A few people still live here, not many." He grimaced guiltily at the camera.

Behind her, Pokey heard the whirr of equipment and someone speaking low into the microphone.

Main Street ended at the bottom of the hill. Directly across, Pokey saw a small red brick building, standing alone on a green.

"That's the fort," Skip Clinton said, beaming at it. "We'll circle around and come back. This way." He turned right and led them past a block of very old, empty buildings, crossed the street, and walked along the side of the last one. "That's it for the town," he said. "Now we'll cut through backyards. Or go to the river first." He waved toward the water, glinting beyond a set of raised railroad tracks.

Andrew, the boy with the thin blond hair, stopped and gazed back toward the railroad station. "The water was over there."

"We have two rivers," Skip Clinton said proudly. "Here, I'll show you."

He led them into an alcove. Beneath a painted sign, RIVER STORY, was a wall full of dusty photographs and charts. A recording came on and a solemn voice began, "The River Story. Two mighty streams, the Potomac and Shenandoah, meet here at Har-"

The recording stopped, silenced by Tom with the flick of a small remote control pack. "Through the backyards will be fine," he said. "We'll get in position." He and Helene jogged off. Skip Clinton looked disappointed.

"Don't want to hear about rivers, I guess. Well —he pointed up to the silent loudspeaker box—"there are

18

lots of recordings hidden around. Put here for visitors to the park long ago. They're heat-sensitive, but not exactly like the TV's we have now. These don't bring instructions or information from headquarters. They just say the same thing, over and over. Recorded." He grinned. "They'll catch you if you get out of line."

The group trailed through backyards. The CCers were on a high porch, filming again. Uneasy, Pokey hugged her waist and kept her head down when she passed below them.

Beyond the last fence was the open green. Skip Clinton put a hand in his pocket. "Here we are, back again. Now I'll show you John Brown's fort."

When they passed the red brick fort, a recorded voice announced from a small pedestal nearby, "On a dark night in the fall of 1859, a band of men—"

It was silenced by Tom.

"Right this way." Skip Clinton crossed a street, opened a door, and everyone trooped in. "This is my museum. Theater's just beyond."

The museum reminded Pokey of long-ago visits to the Smithsonian: display cases filled with dishes and old guns, mannequins in costume, painted models of houses and horses. One wall contained a huge map of the town.

There are the rivers, Pokey thought, tracing them with her finger. *The railroad bridge, the tunnel. And here's where we walked . . .*

In the next room, lights dimmed. Music started. *Late again,* Pokey thought, heading for the door. The way was blocked by Tom and Miss Vanderpugh.

"Read this," Tom whispered. "Right into the mike." Pokey bit her lip and stayed out of their line of vision.

Miss Vanderpugh began, "Another group of children, being entertained at a theater—" She broke off. "But—"

"It's all right," he insisted. "Read it."

" . . . at a theater in Baltimore. The Children's Concern takes as its purpose the welfare and happiness of all. This includes the careful management and well-being of the leftover children."

Miss Vanderpugh stopped speaking. The doors closed. Then she swept out, wringing her hands, her eyes blazing. "Oh-hh! Who do they think they're . . . Pokey!"

"Hi. I . . . I was looking at this map."

"You should be inside."

"I know. But—"

Miss Vanderpugh had started pacing. "They don't give you a minute to look at anything, understand anything. I know."

"Well, they don't."

"Welfare, well-being. Who do they think they're kidding?"

"Are we really going to Baltimore?"

"Baltimore is empty. All the children gone. Fifteen trainloads." She stopped pacing, stood in front of Pokey. "Why do they have to lie?"

Pokey's knees had begun to tremble. "What are they going to do to us?"

Miss Vanderpugh jabbed at her hair, staring at Pokey as if she had at that moment thought of something enormous. Pokey took a step backward. "Pokey, why don't you run away?"

"Huh?"

"Don't let them take you, too."

Pokey stuttered, "Wh-wha—"

Miss Vanderpugh glanced around, noticed a small EXIT door, and opened it. Pokey caught sight of a courtyard. "Do you want to?"

Pokey was paralyzed, rooted to the spot. "I . . . I don't know."

Suddenly, Miss Vanderpugh hurried to her, hugged her tight. "Oh, Pokey, I wish things weren't this way."

Pokey held herself, unyielding. "Will you stay with me?"

"No. I can't." Miss Vanderpugh was not smiling now. "Forgive me. Let's go back."

Pokey didn't move.

"Come on."

Pokey shook her head, thinking of lines and waiting, long corridors, closed faces. And something frightening, she suspected, at the end of the line. "There are lots of hiding places here. Do you think I could?"

"Oh, Pokey. I don't know."

Inside, Helene called, "That's enough. Lights!"

Miss Vanderpugh wiped her eyes, gave Pokey a little shove. "I'd be glad to think of you safe."

Pokey nodded and stepped out into the courtyard. The lights came on in the theater, and Tom ordered, "All right, everybody. Line up."

The old town was full of shadows. Pokey ran to a low wall at the side of the courtyard, held on, and jumped over, banging her knee. She brushed it off, barely feeling pain.

A house nearby had a wide back porch, with steps under it leading to a gloomy basement. Pokey scurried down into the darkest corner under the steps. She crouched there and held her breath.

"This way." Skip Clinton was in the yard. "Here's a shortcut."

"Hi-ho," sang Matron Shrank. "Step it up. We've got a long ride ahead, and it's nearly dark."

CHAPTER TWO

Hannah Lucas's House

FOOTSTEPS FADED, THE TRAIN BELCHED and rumbled. Pokey edged forward. Then with a scream of wheels, the train stopped.

Pokey scurried back to her hiding place.

A woman shouted, loud footsteps rang out. In the distance, one of the heat-sensitive recordings switched on, then another, farther away. Someone thundered into the courtyard, opened a door, crashed into metal. "Damn!"

A distant voice called, "Hey!" and then cried, "Got him! Got one!"

"Over here!" It was Tom, nearby. "Bring him."

Pokey was sure they'd catch her. She shut her eyes and pleaded silently, *No, no . . .*

Lights came on in the courtyard. Pokey wedged deeper into the shadows and listened.

"Found him by the river." Helene was panting. "Andrew, isn't it?"

The boy snuffled as if he was crying. "I was only looking. I . . ." He sniffed again.

Matron cut him off. "What about the girl? Pokey."

"No sign of anybody else," said Helene. "Did you see her, Andrew?"

"N-n-n—" Pokey felt so sorry for him she had to bite a finger to keep from calling out.

"Where's Miss V.?" Tom asked.

"Watching the ones on the train," Helene told him. "Someone has to, or they'll come swarming off like beetles."

"No!" Matron Shrank was angry. "Not my children."

Pokey heard the searchers go again, yelling, setting off recordings. Someone approached her basement. Holding the sweatshirt over her ears, Pokey squeezed herself into the smallest ball, turning her face to the musty wall.

The person walked halfway down, paused a moment, and climbed back up, muttering—it was Matron's voice—"Where could she be? They have to find her. I've never lost a child."

The four reassembled in the courtyard.

"There's a thousand hidey-holes in this place," grumbled Tom.

"Too many," Helene agreed. "Matron, we've got to go."

"I've checked my theater, museum, everywhere," Skip Clinton's voice boomed. "She's not anywhere."

"Of course she is," Matron insisted. "She has to be. We must keep searching."

"Matron, what's one kid more or less?" Tom gave a short laugh. "With all we've got to worry about? There's a whole trainload."

"Yes," agreed his partner. "Let's go."

"No." Matron stood firm. "I will not leave one of my charges behind."

"All right, Matron Shrank." Helene said, businesslike. "You can stay. We'll go."

Skip Clinton burst out, "No! No, ma'am!" He laughed uncomfortably. Pokey could tell he didn't want Matron left behind. "You go on. I'll find her. There are lots of old buildings, bushes by the river. Don't worry. I'll search 'em all. Tomorrow."

"Well . . ." Matron was uncertain.

"River currents," suggested Tom. "She might have drowned."

"Yes." The stationmaster sounded happy. "I'll bet she did."

Pokey suspected they just wanted to be rid of her.

Except Matron. "Yes. Well, Mr. Clinton, you'd better continue the search tonight. The reason we're removing these children," she paused dramatically, "is because of sickness."

"Eh?" asked the stationmaster. "What sickness?"

"Dysentery, cholera," Tom explained. "There are so many new strains, breeding grounds we can't wipe out. Last summer there were epidemics."

"Yes. I heard about that," the stationmaster said smugly. "Wasn't bad out here."

There was a silence. Then Matron Shrank said, "Will you find her?"

"Uh, sure, sure."

"Well, you'd better. There's something more, you see. Something wrong with her immunity."

Pokey raised her head; her breathing tightened. *What? Am I sick?*

"Oh, come on." Helene sounded disgusted.

The stationmaster pounced on Matron's statement. "What do you mean? That Green Mist Disease? What about the others? Do they have it, too? On my streets?"

"No, no," said Tom soothingly. "Don't worry."

Pokey rubbed her chest and stomach. *I don't feel sick.*

"I'll find her. I . . . I . . . I'll get my friend in Brunswick, the stationmaster there. He's got dogs, he'll come and help. I . . . boy, what I wouldn't give for a telephone . . . I'll stand in the circle and rouse headquarters. They'll notify my buddy Wes and he'll be here in no time. We'll catch your kid."

"You do that," said Matron Shrank. "Pokey Hughes is her name."

"I'm in charge in Harpers Ferry. We don't like anything irregular here."

Pokey heard them through a haze of fear mixed with relief. They were leaving!

"Good," said Tom. "You keep the trains running through. That's the main thing."

"Don't you bring those kids on my streets again." His voice diminished. "The naming at the station, I . . . I guess that's all right, but . . ."

The train left. Pokey heard the stationmaster speaking to headquarters. Then even that sound died and she tiptoed up the steps.

The town was dark around her. She didn't know which way to go. Not back to the courtyard. Where were those recordings? Everywhere. She took a few more steps, realizing how absolutely alone she was.

Well, she'd been alone before and knew that time passes if you close your mind, lean against something, breathe.

She touched a corner of a house. There was no sound, no light but a glimmer from the station . . .

It was only a few minutes until she realized she was hearing something new. Another engine, drawing closer. It whistled, downriver. Then, after a moment: barking.

Dogs, coming from Brunswick.

She dashed blindly away from the station, through a

narrow passageway between houses. Main Street was far too exposed, but straight ahead there were wide stone steps, leading upward.

She took a deep breath, ran to them, leaped up two at a time, until a voice stopped her.

"Girl! Hold it!"

She paused.

"There's a recording." It was someone above her. "Stay to the left. Flatten yourself. Careful now."

Pokey did as she was told. The train had reached the station; the dogs howled, still confined.

The voice instructed, "Easy now, come easy . . . Whoa! Now, on that step, slide over . . ." Pokey looked up and saw a shadowy silhouette with hands outspread in warning. "All the way to the right. Softly. This next recording—if it goes on—will tell you about the church, see it?"

Pokey could just make out a looming spire. She stayed to the side and followed the voice up to another, tiny parking lot.

The woman peered at her, grunted, "Ha," in greeting. She was black, old, tall, dressed in layers of worn clothing. "Don't touch me! And don't fall. We've a way to go." She turned and strode across the parking lot, onto a narrow street overhung with branches. The train engine stopped, the hunting dogs' chorus grew more excited.

At a group of houses perched on the edge of a cliff, the woman paused to take a brown-paper package from a fencepost. "Thank you, John," she called. "Can't stop."

The house had a pale light inside, Pokey noticed before hurrying on. She didn't dare slow down or let the old woman out of her sight for an instant.

The dogs were loose now, yelping and calling from several spots in the lower town.

The woman stopped. "Now. You need help."

"I . . . yes. Th-those dogs."

"Stay put. Don't move. I'll be right back."

She wheeled straight up through the underbrush, climbing the hill to the left.

Pokey stayed, quaking. She could hear men hollering to one another, dogs yowling. Were they getting closer?

Then, crashing through the brush, the woman returned, carrying tall fishermen's waders and a blanket.

"So. Get yourself into these boots. Don't touch the outsides." Pokey wiggled into them, tugging them over her shoes. They were huge, wrinkled, and bunched at the tops of her legs with big folds of material to spare. The old woman swirled the blanket around her. "Follow."

Clutching the straps to keep the waders up, Pokey lurched through the bushes. The woman growled, "Hold that quilt together. Keep your scent in. It's not far."

They reached a clearing, a small house set above the town, with light inside.

The woman pushed open the door. "Here." She led Pokey straight through to the kitchen, opened a cabinet under the sink. "Can you fit in there?"

"S-sure."

"Keep the boots on. The quilt tight."

She pushed aside cleansers and soap. Pokey got in. The boots took up a lot of space; it was a tight fit.

"Good." The woman pulled the blanket over Pokey's head. "Don't you move or knock anything down. And don't get scared. The hounds'll smell it." She closed the door.

Oh, brother, Pokey thought. *Not be scared?*

The door opened again. The woman leaned in and smiled. Her dark hair was threaded with gray, her eyes twinkled. "I'm Miss Hannah Lucas. You just tell yourself, 'Hannah's gonna take care of me.' It'll be all right."

Pokey shifted, her knees higher than her head. She was leaning against something damp. "Are they coming?"

"Soon." The door swung shut.

Pokey moved cautiously until she found a position she could hold, and waited. In the next room she heard the woman humming, then dogs outside and a banging at the door.

"Evenin', Miss Hannah. Seen anybody about? We got a runaway."

The answer was firm. "No, Mr. Clinton."

He went right on. "Dogs found the trail in a basement. Chased it halfway up Church Street, then they lost it."

"What kind of runaway?"

"A kid."

"Maybe he turned around. Walked back the way he came."

"She."

"How's that?"

"It's a girl runaway. She. Walked right through my heat-sensitive recordings like they wasn't there. Like you do." He paused. "I'll take a look upstairs, if you don't mind." Pokey heard heavy feet in the kitchen. They climbed stairs, then came back. "OK. Let's look by the river, Wes. She ain't here."

The man outside said something, and Hannah answered, "Help yourself. The water's cool. Don't waste it. I'll mind your dogs."

Terrified, Pokey heard the men come into the kitchen.

Glasses clinked, water roared through the pipes and rushed into the drain. Everything under the sink vibrated. When the water was turned off, the silence was horrible. Pokey breathed into the blanket, repeating silently, *I'm all right. She said I'm all right here.*

Inches away, Wes said, "Can't imagine what happened to my dogs."

Skip Clinton snorted. "Wild goose chase. Maybe she drowned." He sounded hopeful.

"Yeah."

They refilled their glasses, didn't seem in a hurry to move on.

Skip Clinton said, "Boy, those folks wore me out. Chased all over town."

"Better you than me."

"Ha."

They were silent for a while, frighteningly, then Wes asked, "How many people you got left?"

"The same. Miss Lucas here. John McQuarter, the crazy Watson sisters. That's all for Harpers Ferry. There's a couple more in the next town, some strays out in the countryside. Can't budge 'em."

"Brunswick, too. When folks was called to go live in the city, most everybody went. Those that stayed stick like mud. I'm supposed to get rid of 'em. Supposed to get their electric cut off, but . . . nobody tells you how."

Skip Clinton agreed. "Ain't no picnic. Well, man, let's go. When we're done, we can have a *real* drink."

"Righto. What about this old dame?" Wes asked. "She tell the truth?"

"Miss Hannah? Sure. She's a good old darky. Lived here for years."

Pokey was shocked. *The nerve of him.*

Glasses clattered in the sink, the men left. Pokey heard

29

Hannah's footsteps. She was singing low, "Hoooooold on. They'll be back."

And sure enough, a minute later, Skip Clinton burst through a rear door. "Forgot my hat," he announced, clomping around the kitchen. "OK. 'Night, Miss Hannah. Keep a sharp eye out."

"I will," she promised.

Pokey leaned against the drainpipe, raglike. It was a long time before Hannah pulled open the door and whispered, "OK."

Pokey stumbled out stiffly, blinking in the light. "They gone?"

"Yes. They're at the river."

"They'd like it if I drowned."

"Indeed." The woman took hold of Pokey's shoulders. "Here. Let me look at you."

"What's wrong?"

She studied Pokey's eyes, pulled down the lower lids to examine the whites, felt behind her ears and in her armpits. "Stick out your tongue. . . . Hmm. You don't look sick."

"I . . . I don't think I am. But . . ." Pokey took a deep breath. "There might be something wrong with my immunity."

"Yes. So I heard, outside." Hannah peered into Pokey's eyes again, then gently touched her face.

Pokey went on. "I never heard anything about it before. Not from Miss Vanderpugh. Nobody."

"Who was it said that?"

"Matron. She was in charge of our building. She . . . she wanted that man to look for me." Pokey was feeling a little wobbly.

"Skip Clinton. He did act like he had dynamite stuck under him. Where you heading?"

"They're going to Ohio. I . . ." Pokey realized suddenly she had no place to go. "Can I sit down?"

Hannah leaped to action. "You poor child. Of course, sit." She pulled out a chair and Pokey sank into it. "Don't fall asleep now! You hungry?"

Pokey heard the voice from far away. "No-o."

Hannah pulled her to her feet. "You all right? Just sleepy?"

"I'm fine, I think." Pokey swayed. "Just sleepy."

"Better get upstairs, out of sight. I'll tuck you in." Hannah opened a door and pushed Pokey up a narrow stairway to the second floor. The room had a tall bed, a high window, stacks and stacks of boxes and folded cloth. Hannah swept a pile to the floor. "This bed hasn't been used for a long time."

Pokey collapsed gratefully. The last thing she saw was Hannah swatting at a pillow, making dust fly.

Hours later, she woke. Touched her chest, shoulders, cheeks. *I feel all right. . . . Who's there?*

She held her breath and searched the darkness. Hannah was sitting in a chair, rocking slightly. "Didn't want for you to wake and not know where you were."

"Oh." Pokey relaxed a little. "Thank you. Is it morning?"

"Not even deep night. Are you hungry now?"

"Well, yes."

Hannah beckoned, vanished down the steps. Pokey stood, seeing with surprise that she was wearing pink long underwear, tops and bottoms, softer than silk. *Where'd these come from? Her, I guess.*

In the kitchen, Hannah made tea, cut thick slices of homemade bread, and put it all in front of Pokey with a crock of strawberry jam. "No butter, of course." She clucked sadly. "No cow." Then, falling silent, she went

31

to the doorway and leaned there, facing the darkened living room.

Pokey ate, rubbing her bare feet together. She hadn't tasted anything this good for a long, long time. She noticed worn spots on the linoleum, a flower in a jar, a small bedroom leading off the kitchen. The blanket she'd been wrapped in (a faded patchwork quilt) was there, spread neatly on the bed. She swallowed the last bite of bread and cleared her throat.

"Finished?" Hannah took the plate and directed Pokey to the bathroom, a tiny space made from part of the back porch, with shingled walls and a deep bathtub filled with buckets.

Pokey washed her hands, peered at herself worriedly in the mirror, and wiped some jam from her face.

Upstairs again, the woman smoothed the covers under Pokey's chin. "You'll sleep now. I'm going for a little walk. Then I'll be downstairs." She added from the doorway, "You haven't said your name."

"Pokey."

"Ah. Well, good night."

"Thank you," Pokey whispered.

She woke once, thinking she heard voices below. And again later, sure she was hearing music, a harmonica. She thought of Miss Vanderpugh, slipping down corridors, straggles of red hair escaping from her bun. *Wants me to be safe?* Pokey remembered with fear in her heart. *Can I be?*

She turned over, burrowed into the dusty pillow, and sneezed.

As always, when she slept, she didn't dream.

CHAPTER THREE
Out of Line

A STRONG SMELL OF SOMETHING COOKING crept up the stairs and Pokey sat straight up in bed. The room was smaller in daylight with one slanty wall and old things piled everywhere. *What in the world . . . am I doing here?*

It wasn't that she had forgotten. She remembered yesterday, all right.

She got out of bed, tiptoed over to her clothes, folded neatly on a chair. Everything was there but one sock. Holding the clothes in front of herself like a shield, she slipped down the stairs.

Hannah was at the stove, bending over a steaming pot. Fresh carrots and onions spilled over the countertop. The woman was muttering and shaking her head.

Pokey said, "Hi." Hannah turned abruptly, her spoon spraying liquid on the floor. "How are you? What's that?"

"Soup."

"Oh."

They faced each other. *Who is this lady?* Pokey wondered while Hannah scrutinized her with narrowed eyes as if she could read Pokey's face and bones like a book.

Pokey squeezed the bundle of clothes together. "Um, I could only find one sock."

Hannah blinked and smiled. "Yes, I took the other. It's at the riverbank. I made some footprints and . . . left it there." Pokey realized the bottoms of her sneakers were damp and sandy. "Skip will find it. If we're lucky, he'll think you drowned." She went to her bedroom and came back with a pair of men's black dress socks. "Here, wear these."

"Thank you." Hannah was staring at her again. Pokey curled her toes together. "I . . . heard talking in the night."

"John was here. John McQuarter. To see what was happening. He . . ."

Pokey looked up.

"What we want to know is, do you have someplace to . . ." Hannah seemed to think better of the question. She clamped her mouth tight and turned back to the soup pot. "There's a new toothbrush in the bathroom."

"OK." Pokey dressed in the bathroom, folding the black socks over twice so they hardly showed. She brushed her teeth, raked her hair with her fingers (it looked worse than ever), and listened to her thoughts. *She wants me to go away already. Well, OK. I can always go back. Or . . . find someplace alone.*

She shivered. *Think about it later.*

In the kitchen, Hannah said brightly, "Here you are. I didn't even say a proper good morning. How are you? Sleep well?" Pokey nodded, speechless. "Good. Well now, let's sit down and eat breakfast and not worry about anything. We can take care of that later. OK?"

"Sure." Pokey slid into a seat. "That's just what I told myself," she pointed, "in there."

Hannah gave her a funny look. "Hmmh," she said, and brought a teapot, bread, and jam to the table. She sat across from Pokey. "No butter. But I do have canned milk. Want some?"

"No, thank you."

Hannah ate in silence, dunking her bread in her tea, then chewing and chewing. Her hands were the color of old chocolate, brown dusted with gray, with long fingers and bumpy knuckles. Her expression was distant, arrested, as if she was thinking about something miles away.

Pokey fiddled with her bread. "What's in the pot?"

"A chicken."

"A chicken?" She nodded toward the counter. "And you have carrots and onions, too. Where did you get them?"

"John and I—" The woman stopped eating. "Don't you have fresh food in the city?"

"No. It's not safe." Hannah frowned as Pokey went on. "Boxes and cans, they're all right, but nothing else. Because of the green, you know. The poison got on everything."

"You don't grow food? What do you eat?"

"Well, it's hard. There isn't enough, but they found about a million old potatoes and the Food Concern radiated them and they're OK—"

"You eat radioactive potatoes?"

"Yes. Well. They don't hurt us. They just don't taste good." Pokey looked at the stove with suspicion. The bread was heavy in her fingers, uneaten. "So how did you get a chicken?"

"I . . . we . . . took a chance. The poison touched everything. We're all that's left, here together." She held out her hands and shrugged. "So. John McQuarter found a few chickens, nursed them, now he's got a flock. When he kills one, I cook it. That's our arrangement. I picked this one up, last night with you, at his house down on Church Street."

35

Pokey vaguely remembered the tree-lined lane and a brown-wrapped package. "But . . ."

"People here would have starved. Long before John came, the very first autumn after the disaster, I went out and harvested gardens. The tomatoes and onions were huge and healthy, almost as if they'd been fertilized. I carried home what I could, fired up the canning kettle. Gave me something to do. When John came last summer, another growing season was here. Vegetables had seeded themselves and were poking up among the weeds. We searched them out, brought them in. Went through grocery stores, too. We walked for miles after his car ran out of gas."

Pokey touched the rim of her plate. "People are supposed to be in trouble out in the country. And hungry. That's what they say."

"Sometimes I wonder at all the things they say."

"On the TV? Do you hear them?"

"Now and then. There's sets all over town. At Lucy's, and John's. They come on whether you want them to or not—"

"Heat-sensitive."

"—and start yapping at you. Half the time what they say makes mighty small sense."

"Who's Lucy?"

Hannah's face closed and Pokey knew Lucy was gone. "A friend. Are you going to eat?"

Pokey's piece of bread was reduced to fragments. *I ate this food last night . . . Could Matron and everybody be wrong?* Pokey's mouth watered. Fresh food. It was a thing of the past. "That stationmaster, does he eat . . ."

Hannah smiled. "Skip wants both worlds. He takes their cans and, yes, accepts a loaf of bread."

Pokey grimaced and cast her lot. "Can I have a new piece, please?"

"Certainly." Hannah cut two thick slices and passed them over. "I expect you're wondering how it is we have water."

Water was always an issue these days. Taking a nibble, then a bite, Pokey nodded. "How?"

"The first winter . . . after . . ." Hannah bent her head, but didn't stop talking. " . . . after the sickness finally ended, there were a number of people still living here. But also many empty houses. One burned, out a ways, burned clear to the ground. A motor inside, heater or whatever, had turned on and off, on and off. There was nobody to tend it or notice when something went wrong."

"I saw fires," Pokey murmured.

"Well, that's when I thought of the water. I've had frozen pipes, it's no treat. And I said to myself, empty houses? Nobody turning on the furnaces! When it gets cold, the lines will freeze. Now, you know as well as I, ice is thicker than water."

Pokey remembered learning that water expands when it freezes. She nodded, fascinated. She wasn't used to such long conversations anymore and listened, rapt and happy, as Hannah went on.

"The ice gradually pushes out. It can split a metal pipe. I've seen it happen. When warm weather comes, the pipe thaws, and water pours from every break, gushes right out. The thought scared me. For who would see, who would know if a pipe's burst and spraying water in an unused house? How many days would it take, with five—ten—twenty buildings leaking, to drain our tank?"

"I met a girl who said her whole town went dry." Pokey remembered, too, the faucets in her apartment, which

37

often had produced only a tiny stream. "What did you do?"

"I walked out everywhere, found the water meters, and shut them off. It took searching, let me tell you, but I did it. Saved our water."

"Neat. You can't live without water."

"No." Hannah beamed with pride. "John McQuarter climbed up and checked the tank on the hill above town. He says there's a good bit left, and we're careful not to waste it. But . . . I don't know what we'll do when it's gone. It's a long climb up from the river with buckets."

She paused, contemplating her kitchen as if it all might crumble. When her eyes reached Pokey, she was frowning. "Well. I'm going for a walk. Want to come?"

"Um . . . sure."

"I'll be outside." Hannah clattered the dishes into the sink, adjusted the heat under the soup, pulled a battered hat from a peg. "Take your time."

Pokey hesitated for a minute, then followed her to the porch. "What's wrong?"

The old woman was sitting in a ladderback rocker, rocking fast, looking out across the distance to a mountain that rose steeply above a river. She didn't glance at Pokey. "John McQuarter says . . . I make up my own mind, you understand. But John says we have enough trouble."

"I . . ." Pokey didn't mean to be trouble. But she guessed she was.

"I left your sock down there. They'll think you drowned. You can get clean away." Pokey didn't move or speak. "You have people you're meaning to find? Off Charles Town way, maybe?"

"I don't have any people." Pokey kept her eyes on her

feet. *Where could I go?* "If I . . . could I just stay today?"

Hannah rocked harder, glaring at the mountain. Pokey stayed where she was, squeezing her elbows together, head down, as if she could hide herself that way.

"Yes. Of course." Hannah heaved herself up, the chair kept on rocking. "Let's see what Skip does when that train comes back through. You need a sweater?"

"No. But wait. Who . . . who is this John McQuarter?"

"He's my neighbor. Used to be a congressman. You know . . . before. He worked at headquarters, too. But he lives here now." She winked. "We get along because he doesn't ask a thousand questions."

Pokey winced and kept still.

The woman went into the house, then returned wearing a second gray cardigan over the first and new-looking Nike high-tops. "Come on, then. You'll like the river."

She set off down the side of the hill opposite from the way they had come the night before, wound through woods past the corner of an old cemetery, swung onto a rocky trail as if it were flat sidewalk. Pokey scrambled to keep up.

"This is the cliff trail," said Hannah, not slowing down. "There are no houses on this side of Harpers Ferry."

"Or people?"

"Hope not."

The steep path ended at a paved road. "Leads to town. Beware." Hannah left the pavement, crossing a footbridge over a canal into woods again. "That's better."

"What's better?" Pokey bit her tongue. She was trying not to ask questions.

"I always walk easier with plenty of trees around. And ol' Skip's got town habits these days. We should be all right for a while."

"Does he usually bother you?" Pokey asked.

"*He'd* rather we were friendlier."

"Mr. Clinton scares me."

"No doubt. But don't worry. He likes it best when he's sitting in the stationhouse, half drunk or a little more. Gets to feeling real important."

They came to an abandoned railroad track, crossed it, and emerged at the river. It was wide and fast, with rocks protruding like flat backs. "Oh," Pokey whispered, "it's beautiful."

Hannah smiled. "The Shenandoah."

They followed the river to a place where Hannah pointed out footprints. "That's where I left your sock. It's gone." Pokey shifted uncomfortably and moved closer to her companion. They walked on until they could see the town beyond a wide picnic area and a railroad trestle.

Pokey asked, "Is that the same train track?"

"Same as what? It's the one we crossed, back a ways. Not the one you came in on."

Pokey remembered the map in the museum. "The one I came in on goes up the other river."

"That's right. The Potomac. Goes all the way to Cumberland."

"The train goes to Ohio."

"Hmm."

Hannah stopped at a tree whose tangled roots, uncovered by erosion, made a kind of seat. "This is my river-tree. I better rest." She lowered herself and pulled a handkerchief from inside her dress to fan her face.

"Are you OK?"

"Ummhmm. Walking heats you." She took a few deep breaths. "We have a minute. Why don't you go wading. It's cool."

"You, too?"

"No. I'll watch."

Pokey went to the water's edge, threw some rocks, then tossed a twig as far as she could and saw the current catch it. She took off her shoes and black socks and waded out, feeling the sharp stones and squishy mud, the water cold, her feet pink and distorted, tingling.

She squatted, balancing above the surface, her fingers trailing under. The water roared and whispered. Tempted to let her mind drift with it, she began to say the litany, *Remember. We are safe here . . .* and froze in mid-thought. "Safe" was another place, another voice. She wavered, caught her balance. Far too much had happened since yesterday morning; she couldn't drift, or leave so much unspoken.

She splashed back to Hannah and said, "Did you see Andrew? He came here, to the river. They almost left him, too."

"No. From where I stood I couldn't see the river."

Pokey wondered where he was, where they all were. Being out of line, out of the constant closeness and movement, was frightening. She'd like to tell Miss Vanderpugh that.

"Miss Vanderpugh said, 'Hide.' "

"What are they doing with you, all you children?"

"They take care of us." Pokey knelt, her fingers brushing the ground. "They don't really explain things. But I know there's too many kids. Summer is even worse than winter, what with bugs and smells and epidemics. The Children's Concern has a lot to worry about. They take care of that."

Hannah didn't answer. "There are too many kids," Pokey repeated. "We stay in government buildings, on the mall in Washington. There were more of us, you know, left after . . ."

"Yes. Here, too. We kept them in the hotel for a while. Now they've gone to live in the city. We are all supposed to, all us survivors."

"Who says so?"

"Skip's bosses, the TV people. We'll be safer, they say, kept together. They're getting things started again and there's . . . danger." She shook her head, her mouth pursed. "I disagree."

"Really?"

"Oh, don't mind me. I'm just an old woman." She smoothed the soft blue fabric of her dress over her knees. "They came here, one bunch, the first spring . . . after. Three men and two women. Put Skip in charge of the train station while they got the electric plant started again. It's hydroelectric, runs by water, and makes power for the city. When they left, the children and most everybody else went along, too." She looked hard at Pokey. "Those people called themselves . . ."

"The Children's Concern."

"Yes. Were they good to you?"

"I . . . guess." She remembered days passing, all the same. Gray food and warm beds. "We . . . were so sad."

"Were those your teachers, the people I saw you with?"

"We don't have real teachers."

"The red-headed woman, the other one that looks like a battleship—"

Pokey grinned. "That's Matron Shrank."

"And the two with the fancy equipment."

"Tom and Helene. They were making a videotape to show on TV. So people would . . . would be fooled. Miss Vanderpugh said, 'Why do they lie?' " Pokey fell silent.

The sound of the river, the dappled rush of the current, made yesterday seem unreal.

Hannah gazed out across the water and said, "I've watched those trains. Don't like the look of 'em. The children are so still, the adults so . . . tight." Hannah leaned forward, her hands on her knees. "And you? What's your history?"

"Me? It's nothing." Pokey brushed her feet and pulled on her shoes and socks. She couldn't come out with things the way Hannah did. She looked at the river, so she wouldn't forget how it glittered and nudged the muddy bank. "Anyway, I'll be gone tomorrow."

"Pah!" Hannah stood up. "We'll see about that. Hurry now. We better not miss that train." She led Pokey through the trees, under the railroad trestle, to the alcove marked RIVER STORY. Showed Pokey how to slide against the wall, out of reach of the recording's sensors. They traveled on, through backyards, to the last fence before the open green.

"That's John Brown's fort," Pokey whispered. "They told us yesterday."

"Right." Hannah held a finger to her lips. "It's all Skip Clinton's territory now. Stay behind me." She crossed the green to a corner of the fort, held out a hand, motioning Pokey to stay, and headed toward a tall flight of cement steps leading up to the railroad station.

A bell rang: *Ding-ding-ding-ding.*

Hannah made a broad gesture with her left arm: *Come on!*

Pokey ran. She dashed straight for Hannah, too close to an information pedestal with a loud recording that switched on, proclaiming "On a dark night in the fall of . . ."

Pokey stumbled. Hannah froze, then hissed, "Into the bushes." Pokey dove into thorns as feet thundered overhead.

Hannah, halfway up the stairs called, "Yoo-hoo! Mr. Clinton? Is that you?"

"Ha-han—" He was out of breath. "Hannah Lucas? That you?"

"Lord, I'm sorry." She sounded a little foolish. "I wasn't thinking. Walked right into that thing. I was so worried, wondering about that runaway you told me about. You catch her?"

"Yep. Done drownded. Found her clothes by the river."

"Oh, my."

"You go on home now, Miss Hannah. I got a train coming."

"OK, Mr. Clinton. See you later."

Pokey heard him go away. Hannah pattered down the steps, speaking as if to herself. "Easy now. Let's go. Right up the street. You stay in the bushes to the side."

The street paralleled the main tracks and stationhouse, but ten feet lower; Pokey could creep along without being seen. Still, she jumped when the stationmaster hollered, "Miss Hannah? You there?"

"Yes?"

"Why don't you come over later. We could have a cup of tea or a glass of beer. Game of cards."

"Oh, I'm sorry, Mr. Clinton," she called back. "Not today. I've got a load of washing to do."

Near the driveway that led to the station, Hannah darted across to a small wooden stairway that climbed between houses to Main Street. She shooed Pokey partway up, then whispered, "Stop. We can see the train from here."

44

"Are . . . are there any recordings?"

"No. Scared you, huh?"

Far upriver a whistle blew, then the ground shook, the train tooted again, rumbled into view, and stopped.

It was nearly empty.

Tom and Helene were in front with the engineer. Skip Clinton spoke to them, then hurried back and handed Pokey's white crew sock to Matron Shrank, standing by an open door. Behind her, Miss Vanderpugh suddenly put her hands to her face and turned away.

"Look there," Hannah said.

"Where?"

The train was shining silver. With a strange blue and orange blob skittering backward on top of the last car.

"It's somebody," Pokey whispered.

The person got to the end, careened off, and slipped to the ground. Then he crouched, wavered, and ran for the parking lot. Ran crookedly, with a limp. It was a teenage boy in an orange T-shirt and jeans.

He staggered and collapsed.

Hannah asked, "Is that your Andrew?"

"No. I've never seen him before."

CHAPTER FOUR
Menfolk

 THE TRAIN LEFT, THE DOOR TO THE STA-tionhouse slammed. Pokey watched the spot where the boy had disappeared.

With an enormous sigh, Hannah took a step downward. "Well, let's get it over with."

"Get what over with?"

"We can't just leave him there for Skip to find."

Pokey felt weak in the stomach. "I guess you're right."

They found the boy crumpled, unmoving, between a van and a car, half on his side, one hand flung over his head. He was breathing heavily.

At Hannah's touch, he rolled over. His mouth was open, his eyelashes thick and dark and very beautiful. Pokey frowned. His hands were clenched, the palms bloody.

Hannah brushed his cheek. "He's got fever."

"He's sick?"

"Burning up." She hoisted him from one side. "Come on. Let's get him home."

They lugged him a little way, then froze as from the station a voice called, "Clinton? Skip Clinton. Do you hear me? Step onto the mark, please. Clinton? Clinton!"

Hannah hissed, "Stay down. They're calling him."

46

The warning was unnecessary, Pokey was practically flat on the pavement, clutching the boy's arm.

A door banged and Skip Clinton answered, "Yes, yes. What is it? Here I am."

"Clinton? Ah, now I see you—" Without realizing what she was doing, Pokey rose up and peered around a fender, through windshields and side glass, and saw the stationmaster staring up at the TV camera.

Hannah yanked her down. "Careful, you fool!" The boy's eyes opened in surprise.

The man from headquarters went on, "Did that train come back through?"

"Yes, indeedy. A few minutes ago."

"Good. You find that kid?"

"I made a full report to the Children's Concerners on the train. The lost person is all accounted for. Drownded. You don't need to worry about Harpers Ferry anymore."

"Right. OK. We put an extra query into the files by your name. It'll tell us if there's anything unusual there. Help you out."

"You don't need to. I tell you, it's all taken care of."

"We're helping you, Clinton. That's all. Over and out."

The boy was struggling. Hannah put her hand over his mouth and whispered in his face, "Quiet. Don't let *him* catch you." The stationhouse door slammed. The boy was trying to scream. Then his eyes rolled up and he went limp.

Hannah touched his cheek. "He's breathing. Fainted. Come on, let's get him home."

Heads down, they dragged him through the parking lot, then bumped up the wooden steps, across Main Street, through a steep yard to Church Street, and on up the path to Hannah's.

Hannah kicked open the door and went straight

through to her bedroom. "Easy now, let him down." She threw back the quilt and they got him into bed.

He roused briefly, groaned, "Uh-hhh."

"Shh," said Hannah, smoothing the hair back from his face. "Go to sleep." Bending, she stripped off his clothes (Pokey averted her eyes) and pulled the sheet over him in just his T-shirt and jockey shorts.

"What . . . what's wrong with him?" Pokey asked.

Hannah pulled down his lower lids, felt behind his ears and in his armpits. "Some kind of fever. Infection. I'm no doctor. Magician either. I don't know yet." She pressed his stomach, then laid her hand on his chest. Pokey still hadn't moved. "What's wrong with you?"

"Nothing." She fled to the kitchen.

"It's not the same sickness, girl," Hannah assured her, standing in the doorway between the two rooms. "Don't you understand?"

"I . . . sure. I'm sorry."

"We'll figure out what's wrong with him. But now let him rest. Maybe we can get that soup made." She brought the carrots and onions to the table. "Chicken's over-cooked. Here, can you cut the vegetables?"

Pokey nodded and picked up an onion. Hannah piled the pieces of chicken on a plate and carried it, steaming, to the table. She took a seat at the far end so she could see the bedroom. "I'll get you some turnips, too. Try to make them look like celery."

"Why? Don't you have any?"

"You need celery to make a good chicken soup. But, no, I don't have any."

"Is there a peeler for the carrots?"

"In the top drawer."

Carefully avoiding the bedroom door, Pokey found

the peeler and began skinning a carrot. "Matron took away people who weren't well. We were supposed to never think about it."

"Hmh! People are always going to get sick. That's stupid."

Pokey ducked her head (nobody ever called Matron Shrank stupid) and started making long strokes on the carrot. She couldn't hold back memory.

Six days after the green cloud dissipated, Pokey's parents fell ill. Weak and wheezing, her father said, "I'm going to try to get us to Fairfax Hospital while I can still drive. They have serum there." (That wasn't true. She found out later it was one of the rumors that had spread like fire.)

Her mother's eyes were green. She was too faint to stand without holding a chair or tabletop. "Take care of Jimmy, honey. Mrs. Beasley will look in on you. We . . . we'll try to get back."

That was the last Pokey saw of them.

Jimmy was a good baby. Pokey changed his diapers, gave him food. She missed her parents terribly and for a long time clung to the possibility that they would return. Mrs. Beasley came over from next door and told her, "When people get this thing, they don't get better. There's no hiding from the fact." Then Mrs. Beasley had trouble moving and breathing. She went to the Red Cross clinic at the junior high school and that was that: she was gone, too.

Terrified, Pokey stayed in the apartment, took care of Jimmy, in a slow-moving state close to tears. Eight days later, the Pampers and canned milk gone, she put him in the stroller and went out. The few people they passed looked haunted, furtive. In the Safeway, she picked out what they needed. There was no one to take her money; no one was looting just then, or breaking things; no one was there at all.

When they got home, Jimmy laughed and climbed on her stomach, beating her chest like a drum, yelling, "Po-po-po," for Pokey.

When he got sick she wanted to die as well. . . .

She'd been peeling a carrot all in one place, it was swaybacked with long woody streaks exposed. She turned it and did the other sides, then worked on the rest until they were finished and there was a tumble of bright skins on the table.

Hannah had dissected the chicken. Before her were piles of bones, skin, and meat. "I'll give the skins to the cat and bury the bones in the compost. Of course, she'll dig them up. She doesn't miss much."

Pokey couldn't be so easily distracted. "My brother died." Hannah clucked in sympathy but Pokey didn't look at her. "I took him to the Red Cross clinic at the junior high. They said there wasn't any medicine, but they gave us something to help him sleep and a cot in the biology lab. I stayed with him . . ." Hannah nodded, her eyes big with understanding.

"After he died, they said they would take him away. There were big trucks hauling the corpses. I wouldn't let them. I wrapped him in a blanket"—she swallowed hard and hurried on—"and carried him out to the street. There were lots of people there because of the clinic, cars and confusion. I . . . I waited and after a while a man came out, carrying a lady wrapped up like Jimmy. I said, 'Mister, where you going?' He looked at me a minute and said, 'Come on.'

50

"We loaded them both in the back of a station wagon and drove out to the country and found a farm—there was no one there—and we buried them in an apple orchard. The man drove a backhoe to dig the hole. I . . . put three rocks on Jimmy's grave and my turquoise ring. It was all I had. The man drove me home and squeezed my hand and said, 'Even this won't last forever.' He wanted to help me more but I said no." She fell silent. She had never told this tale before and it seemed to shimmer in the air between them.

Hannah was shaking her head. "Poor baby."

Pokey pushed the memory away. "They took the bodies to the south in trucks and cremated them. There was smoke for days and days—"

"Here, too."

"I stayed where I couldn't see it. I wished I'd get sick. I didn't care." Pokey nudged the pile of carrots. *Is the sickness coming back? Does he have it? Do I?*

Apparently following her own thoughts, Hannah said, "That disease was a nightmare. Thank God it's gone."

Pokey held her breath. "Are you sure?"

"Yes, indeed. John says so, too."

"But Matron—"

"That woman will say anything to get people to do what she wants. Isn't that so?" Pokey nodded, uncertain. "The Green Mist Disease can't come back. We've got plenty of troubles, but that isn't one of them."

Somewhat reassured, Pokey got three turnips from the sink and began cutting them into squares like chopped celery.

"No!" the boy shouted from the bedroom. Hannah jumped up and ran to him; Pokey too, as far as the door. He was sitting up, tangled in the sheet. "Where . . . where . . . ?"

Hannah leaned over him, saying with great dignity, "I am Miss Hannah Lucas. You are at my home in Harpers Ferry. I will care for you."

He fell back against the pillows, an arm across his eyes. "Ohhhhh."

Hannah was all business. "Come now. Let me look at you. Can you talk?"

He eased his arm down, his eyes bright with fever. "Y-yes."

"Where do you hurt?"

"I—I'm so hot. My head hurts, my eyes. I want to sleep. . . ."

"What else?"

"My throat."

"Ah." Hannah smiled. "I'll have a look." Her capable hands touched his forehead, under the ears, his stomach, probing and soothing. "Pokey, get me the flashlight, on the dresser."

Pokey did and Hannah ordered, "Open wide. Stick out your tongue. Say, 'Ahhhh.' "

"Ugggg," he groaned.

"Wider. Stick out your tongue." She squinted, exclaimed, "Mph!" and switched off the flashlight.

He looked worried. "What is it?"

"Disgusting. Red streaky throat. Huge tonsils. Could be strep. You're sick, boy."

"I know. I . . ." He gazed at the room. "How did I get here?"

"You rode a train," Pokey said. "On *top*."

He lifted his still-clenched hands, moving the fingers a little, and touched the raw places. "I couldn't let go. I'd be a goner. They—" His voice broke.

"How long's it been since you ate?" Hannah asked.

"I—I don't know."

52

"I'll get you something. Pokey, stay here."

Hannah went to the kitchen and Pokey tiptoed closer to the bed. "What's your name?"

He was looking at the far corner of the room and hardly seemed to hear. "Ross."

"Where you going?"

"Washington." He closed his eyes. Pokey didn't think he should go to sleep again. "Where'd you come from?"

"Denver . . . and Iowa."

"Did you see a bunch of kids? Were you in Ohio?"

He covered his face, moaning, "No. No, no."

"Shh. Never mind. It's all right."

Hannah came hurrying in with a tray of food. "Here you are, stewed tomatoes and bread."

Ross licked his lips. "I—I don't think I can eat."

"Sure you can. The first bites are always the worst." Pokey held the tray while Hannah pulled Ross to a sitting position and propped pillows behind him. "There. Now, try a little."

He took a small spoonful of tomatoes, grimaced, and swallowed.

"Fine," said Hannah. "Keep it up."

Pokey retreated to a corner of the room. He ate almost all the tomatoes and the insides, but not the crusts, of bread. "That's all. Wonderful," he said, and sagged under the covers.

"Wait a minute. Don't sleep yet. I want you to take some aspirin. And Pokey will get you medicine." ("Me?" Pokey squeaked, unnoticed.) "You ever take penicillin?"

"Y-yes. I took some in Iowa, until I felt better. I did feel better, honest. For a while." He winced when he swallowed the aspirin, then grinned and curled up on his side. "Mmmmm."

Hannah carried the tray back to the kitchen. Pokey

stayed and watched him, wary. *Why did he get upset when I mentioned Ohio?*

"Pssst!" Hannah motioned from the kitchen.

Pokey tiptoed to her. "I found out one thing. His name is Ross."

"Good. Now listen. You'll have to go down to John's and get the medicine."

"But—"

"I'll stay here in case he wakes. Get this soup finished."

"But J—"

"Tell him we've got somebody sick here and we need help. He'll listen."

"Won't he tell on me? Tell Skip Clinton?"

"No. He promised. Last night."

"But he wants to send me away."

"You just tell him I said you're staying."

Pokey blinked. *Huh?*

Hannah explained how to describe Ross's illness, then said, "The house is the middle one on Church Street. Where I got the chicken. Keep an eye out for Skip, but he's rarely there."

"Are you sure?"

"Stand firm. You can do it. Now, go on."

"O . . . K." Pokey ran out, dropped to a walk on the path, slowing even more when she got to Church Street.

Well, here goes, she thought, marching to the door of the middle house. Her knock seemed frail. She knocked again, louder, then peeked in a side window. Nobody was there.

But someone was making noise around back.

Cautiously, she snuck along the walk beside the house and stopped at the rear corner. There was a man in khaki pants and a flannel shirt working in a patch of garden. He was kneeling in the dirt, patting earth around a green young plant. Then he got up, picked up a wooden stake, and began pounding it into the ground by the seedling.

Pokey took a deep breath and squeezed her fingernails into her palms. "Hi."

John McQuarter jumped, then glared at her. "You still here?"

Don't be scared, she told herself. *He looks like Uncle Jerry, sort of tall and important, like a wrinkled movie star.* She began, "Um, yes. I . . ." and was tongue-tied.

He dropped his hammer and walked up the back steps and into the house.

"Hey! Wait!" Pokey cried. "Hannah says—" She couldn't let him get away. She ran after him, up the steps and into the kitchen.

He was standing in the middle of the room, his arms crossed. "You seem determined to speak to me."

Pokey gulped. "You have to help us. Hannah said." He turned to the sink and washed his hands as she continued. "We've got trouble. A boy. He's sick."

"I saw."

Oh, really? And what else did you see? Me, last night? From his backyard John McQuarter had a good view of the lower town. It made her mad to think of him watching her and not helping. *My Uncle Jerry wouldn't do that.* She clenched her mouth, narrowed her eyes, and outwaited him.

"So?" he finally said. "What do you want?"

"Hannah says you keep the medicine."

"Yes."

"He's fifteen or sixteen. Middle-sized. She said it might be strep. Tonsillitis. He took penicillin before and it got better but he quit too soon."

"Very well." He went into the next room where he

55

pulled several books from the shelves and began reading first one, then another, muttering. Then he turned to her.

"Penicillin again, I guess. Go upstairs, second door on the right. In cupboard number four you'll find bottles of two-hundred-fifty-milligram tablets. He should take"—he consulted the book again—"one every six hours. Let me see . . ." He multiplied in his head. "Get forty tablets altogether. He has to keep it up for ten days. He can get rheumatic fever and damage his heart if he doesn't. Who is he?"

"He's from Denver. Are you . . . a doctor?"

He put the books back on the shelves, his expression almost pleasant. "No. Hannah and I cleared out some pharmacies and doctors' offices. We put together enough to get by, on the easy things. We neither one of us do surgery."

"Mmm," she said, not sure if he was kidding. She could see from the crowded bookshelves he had cleared out a library as well.

"If you'll excuse me, Miss . . ."

"Hughes," she said politely.

"Get!"

"Yes . . . sir." She ran up the stairs.

The room was like a small drugstore, with neat rows of Epsom salts, headache remedies, bandages. Prescription powders and pills were in numbered glass-fronted cabinets marked CAREFUL! Three refrigerators stood against the wall, humming.

Pokey found the medicine, counted out forty pills, and put them in a plastic bottle.

Across the hall, she couldn't resist an open door. It was a sitting room, with comfortable chairs and a big

TV. She ducked out before the set could sense her presence and come to life.

There was no sign of John McQuarter downstairs or outside.

Pokey clutched the pill bottle and ran back uphill, worrying. *Boy, that guy's tough. Hannah said, "Tell him you're staying." What did she mean by that? Am I? Should I?*

And Ross. What about him?

CHAPTER FIVE

"Remember. We Are Safe Here..."

THE SOUP WAS COOLING IN JARS ON THE counter. Pokey and Hannah ate lunch (bread and stewed tomatoes, same as Ross), not talking much, just listening for any sound from the bedroom. Pokey was trying to be no trouble, sitting very still and barely clanking her spoon in her bowl. Hannah seemed deep in thought.

When the dishes were dried and put away she smiled at Pokey. "Fetch your bedclothes. We'll air 'em out."

"OK." Pokey pulled the blankets from her bed, grabbed the pillows, and staggered downstairs and outside with the heavy load. Hannah spread everything on the clothesline and picked up two stout sticks.

"Watch me," she said and banged a blanket. *Whump!* A cloud rose. Hannah stepped back. "Good thing plain old dirt isn't poison." She hit the blanket again and a pillow bounced to the ground.

"Let me." Pokey held her stick like a baseball bat and waited while Hannah clamped a corner of the pillow to the line. Then she wound up. *Whack! Whack!*

Dust flew, glittery in the sunlight. Pokey grinned and kept on. *Whack! Whack! Whack!*

"Easy," said Hannah. "You'll have them in shreds."

Pokey wound up, then, realizing what Hannah had said, struck at half strength. "Sorry."

Hannah nodded and hit the blanket, not a lot more softly. They continued, alternating *Whump, Whack,* in easy rhythm until Hannah stopped and leaned on her stick, staring across the distance at the sheer, cliff-faced mountain. Pokey balanced her stick in two hands, sensing something was coming.

"Well," the woman began.

"Hmm?"

"I expect you're wondering about what I said this morning. About you leaving."

Pokey tried to make herself small, still half-expecting to be sent away.

"Well, you can quit worrying. John thought it would be best. But he doesn't know everything." Her eyes flashed. "I'm not one to run from trouble. Now there's more of it."

Pokey nodded toward the house. "You mean him."

"I mean you can stay here for a while. Fix up that room. Get comfortable." She reached out and touched Pokey's shoulder. "From what you said, you can use a little comfort. I'll get some sheets," she added, and went back into the house.

Oh. Oh, my. Stay? Longer than . . . tomorrow? Pokey took down the pillows and blankets and trailed inside, her thoughts disintegrating.

Hannah handed her clean white sheets from the cupboard near the bedroom. "Here. Use anything you find up there. Move furniture, change whatever you like."

"OK."

Pokey made the bed with perfect hospital corners the way Miss Vanderpugh had taught her, then hesitated.

The room contained a jumble of chairs, chests, old mixers, clocks, radios. Everything was covered with piles of folded fabric, draperies, linens. Just looking made Pokey's nose wrinkle.

She didn't feel secure enough to stake out a real claim. *But I could,* she told herself, *get rid of the sneezy stuff.*

The room on the other side of the stairway was smaller, darker, even more of a storeroom, with old pictures teetering on boxes, furniture looming; it all seemed forgotten.

How long's she lived here, anyway?

Gingerly at first, then with increasing sureness, Pokey moved the piles of draperies, sweaters, and washed-out blankets.

She opened a box labeled SAM's. The contents were so well folded they made her pause: men's work clothes, washed a thousand times and nice to touch. Tough old denims, soft gray pants, collarless shirts. She put the box on a table by itself and went back for one last thing, a plastic bag marked WOOLENS. A faint smell of mothballs leaked out when she touched it and stayed in the air even in the farthest corner of the far room.

There. That's enough.

She retreated to the bed, took off her shoes and socks, and sat cross-legged, rubbing her toes.

Should I really stay?

Not used to choices, or private space, she held on to her feet, rocking slightly, the way Trudy had.

I miss the others, all the kids. I wonder what they're doing. She didn't know about Ohio, but in Washington they'd be peeling potatoes.

Am I really safer here? I like it, but it's scary, being . . . out loose like this. Nobody tells you what to do.

She thought of Matron Shrank, solid, certain, and the

daily litany: "Remember. We have lived through a terrible time. . . ."

The part we say, it's . . . good for anywhere, Pokey thought. *Remember. We are safe here. All things are temporary. Remember we are safe here. Safe . . .*

She recited the words over and over in her mind until Hannah called, "Hello? Finished?" and appeared in the doorway.

Pokey blinked, getting back to the present.

"It's looking better." Hannah swept some of the remaining clutter into a corner, pushed the easy chair to an angle with the bed, brought forward a chest of drawers, scattering its contents. "Here. It's empty." She banged the drawers to be sure. "You can keep your things in this."

Pokey didn't have any "things." "How long have you lived here?"

"More than fifty years. I came to go to school; one of the first Negro colleges was here. Fell in love before I could finish . . . with Sam Lucas, who went riding by every day in his wagon. Lord, he was beautiful." She let out a big sigh. "If I'd hauled some of this to the dump when I had the chance, you wouldn't be asking so many questions. I think there's a mirror somewhere . . ." She went into the adjoining room, came back with a scratched mirror, and hung it on a nail near but not quite above the chest. "Good."

"Th-thank you."

"Find yourself a rug. Clean this chair a bit." She gave a couple of swats to the easy chair, sending up a cloud of dust. "Whew! There's a lamp in the other room. You'll have to run a wire from the light bulb in the ceiling."

"But how?"

"You'll find a dishpan of electrical plugs and such"—

61

she gestured—"in there. I'm going up the street now."

"Wh-where?" Pokey felt like she'd forgotten how to talk right.

"Just to Lucy's. It's sort of my"—she shrugged helplessly—"pantry. I know, I have room here, too. Anyway, Ross is sleeping. Listen for him, hmm?"

"Sure."

At the stairs, Hannah turned and beamed at the transformed room. "Nice up here."

Pokey smiled despite herself, too shy to speak. She waited until she heard Hannah leave, then hurried to the other room where she'd noticed a rolled-up braided rug and a squatty pink lamp. Humming, she spread the rug near her bed, set the lamp on the chest, and ran back to search for an extension cord. "Ouch!" She'd banged into a table, stubbed her toe, and knocked an old metal coffeepot to the floor, scattering the parts everywhere.

"Ow!" she cried, hopping on one bare foot and holding the other.

She retrieved the coffeepot and was trying to fit the pieces together when she heard a crash downstairs and someone yelling. "No! Please!"

Oh, no. They've caught him.

Frightened, she ran to the steps. Heard nothing. Snuck down. The stairs creaked; her knees trembled. She opened the door a crack and saw Ross, wrapped in a sheet, shrinking away from her.

"No," he croaked, "don't take me." He ran from her, waving his arms, and collided with a doorway. "No! Please!" he shrieked again as Pokey touched him.

"Sh-h. It's all right." She took hold of his arm and led him back toward the bedroom. "What's wrong?"

He pointed to the ceiling, speechless.

"That was me."

Wild-eyed, out of breath, he sputtered, "Those kids . . . the beds. They're coming."

"No, no. Who? No one knows you're here."

He stopped. He was taller than she was, and stronger. If he didn't want to move, it was like trying to shove a house. Nothing happened.

"Who?" he echoed. "I . . ." He closed his eyes and shuddered violently. She pushed and he started walking, all the way to the bed where he sank down, glancing in fear at the ceiling.

"Who . . . was that?"

"Me. I dropped something. Stubbed my toe." She held out a bare foot to show him. "See? I'm sorry."

"It was you? You're sure?"

"Sure, I'm sure." He was sitting on the ends of the sheet, his arms pinned. "You should get untangled. Here." She tugged at an edge.

He shifted, pulling the sheet loose, turned over and leaned against the pillows. "I hate to be sick."

"I know."

"And"—he was shaking his head, his eyes closed—"I don't want to think about things. Talk to me."

Pokey had no idea what to say. "OK. Um, how do you feel?"

"Awful."

"I can tell." Now she was speechless.

"Where is that lady?"

"She had to go for a walk. Don't worry. I'll stay with you."

He nodded, smiling weakly. "Talk to me. Tell me something. Then I'll feel better."

"Well . . ." She walked over and stood by the bottom corner of the bed. "I'll tell you something you can say to yourself to make you feel better. It works. Really."

"What's that?"

She sat on the edge of the bed, folded her hands, and explained, "You say these words, over and over: Remember. We are safe here. All things are tempo—"

"No," he whispered. He was dead-white and terrified. *"You."*

"Me? What?" He was tense as a cornered animal, his glance darting. "What's wrong?"

"You won't get me." He leaped out of bed and ran for the kitchen. Pokey chased him, tackled him, and knocked him down. He groaned, "Oooooogh," and fainted.

Pokey stood over him. *What was that about? What am I supposed to do?*

She stayed where she was, for fifteen long minutes, afraid to touch or try to move him, until Hannah returned.

"What's this?" she demanded, dropping some bundles. "What happened?"

"I . . . I scared him. First I dropped a coffeepot. Then . . ."

"Huh," said Hannah, puzzled. "Well, come on, let's get him back to bed." She lifted one side. Pokey moved to take the other, but at Hannah's touch, Ross opened his eyes, looked at Pokey, and screamed. Hannah took it in and said, "Come on, boy. Pokey, stay out there."

She heard the bedsprings creak, Hannah speaking, Ross answering. She couldn't make out the words. Then Hannah came back.

"You scared him, girl."

"I told you."

64

"What did you say?"

"I . . . I told him something Matron used to have us say. To make us feel safer. I . . ." She didn't want to repeat the words, didn't want to say them out loud. "I can't imagine why it scared him. He looked at me like I was a monster or something."

Hannah shook her head. "Well, he's resting now. You . . . stay out of his sight for a while. Here, let me show you what I brought." Grinning suddenly, she emptied the contents of a large paper bag onto the kitchen table. "For you."

"Me?" said Pokey. "Really?"

"Yes, indeed."

It was a wardrobe, her size. Calvin Klein jeans, a purple crewneck, several T-shirts and blouses, long flannel nightgowns, four pairs of bright pink-and-aqua-striped underwear. All worn, but in good condition.

"Who . . . whose were they?"

"Lucy's child. She outgrew them, and the little one—" Hannah broke off, then said quickly, "was too little. They were being saved for her."

Pokey touched a fold with a fingertip, as if the cloth were hot enough to burn. She had worn used clothes before: from the bins at the IRS. They were anonymous. But these—she could almost see a laughing girl. She didn't think she could bear to use them.

"Go on," said Hannah. "You don't have a thing but what you've got on."

Pokey carried the garments upstairs and shoved them into the back of the bottom drawer of her chest. *I'll stay in my own shorts till they rot,* she told herself. Then with a start she remembered the box marked SAM's.

These are only a little big, she thought, holding a pair of trousers to her waist. She put three pairs of soft gray pants into the bottom drawer, closing off sight of Lucy's daughter's purple sweater, filled the middle drawer with pale, striped shirts. In the top she placed Hannah's pink long underwear, her one sock, a stretchy gold belt, and a long silk scarf she'd found.

There.

She hooked up her lamp and looked at the room. *It really is nice,* she thought, and smiling, went downstairs. Hannah was sweeping the kitchen floor.

"I found some pants and stuff in a box. Can I have them, too?"

"Yes, anything," Hannah said. "Soup needs to go down to John's. Will you take it?"

"Um, sure." Pokey didn't particularly want to see John McQuarter again, but she knew she couldn't refuse.

Hannah wrapped two jars with a dishtowel and put them in the brown paper bag. "Hold it from the bottom."

"OK."

It was bright and clear, late afternoon. The soup reached through its wrappings and warmed her stomach. Far off, she heard a bird. She stopped to listen but it didn't sing again. *That was a bird. But Matron said they all died. Not only that . . . here I am, carrying fresh food around, eating it like I never heard a warning. Well, it's . . . better. Matron and the others—they sure didn't know everything.*

John McQuarter wasn't home.

"Hello?" she called from the kitchen. Her voice echoed and died. She left the soup bag on the counter and, without knowing she meant to, went upstairs to the room with the TV and stood near the blank screen, letting the mechanism sense her.

The set flickered to life, showing a man at a desk littered with papers.

He read, " . . . day's announcements. We have centralized care and safety. We all do our part. There is
solace in work. Remember. We are safe here. All things
are temporary. . . .

"Electrical production is at a low level. Conserve. New
operations require more every day. Therefore, random
use is being eliminated. All power is being withdrawn
from the outlying areas so it will not be wasted. If *you*
are in an outlying area, come into the city. We cannot
guarantee your safety otherwise. I repeat, if you are not
authorized by central headquarters you will lose
power. . . ."

What? Pokey wondered, *Is John McQuarter authorized?
Or Hannah? I guess Skip Clinton is.*

"All services to Annapolis and the eastern shore are
being discontinued. Survivors are urged to make their
way to Route Fifty where flares have been placed along
the highway. Send off a flare and wait for pickup. Send
off a flare and hope for pickup. . . .

"Food service will be one hour late in Areas Two and
Three. I repeat, food service is available today in all
areas, with a one-hour delay in Areas Two and Three.
Bring a bowl. . . ."

I know what that means. Potato soup.

"There have been reports of bad water. Be careful.
Drink only from certified sources. We must be vigilant.
New germ strains of virus and bacteria thrive in warm
weather. We are doing all possible to avoid a recurrence
of last summer's epidemics. Drink only from certified
sources. . . .

"Avoid emergencies. Health care is in short supply. . . ."

Everything is in short supply. In D.C.

67

"We have no new reports of visitors from beyond the Washington area, but we are watchful and concerned. No news isn't good news, not these days. . . .

"The Children's Concern reports excellent progress in caring for the leftover children. Films of their latest field trips will be shown soon. . . ."

That's us, I guess.

"Remember. We are safe here. We are rebuilding. We will take care of you. Do your part. . . .

"Hello. Here are today's announcements. We have centralized care and—"

The tape would repeat now. Pokey covered her ears (it always took a while for a set's sensors to give up on you) and hurried outside.

She was so happy to be away from the announcer's voice, away from the city and its instructions and worries, that she stood on the back porch and yelled, "Soup!" John McQuarter's chickens set up a frightened squawking behind their fence. Pokey clapped a hand over her mouth. *Careful, dummy,* she scolded herself, and scooted back to Hannah's.

CHAPTER SIX
High Voltage

 POKEY STAYED IN THE KITCHEN, QUIETER than a mouse so she wouldn't frighten Ross, until after supper. Then Hannah whispered, "Don't move," and went into the bedroom. "Come on, Ross boy. Time for the bathroom."

Pokey stood by the stove, trying to look natural, but he jumped when he saw her. "You," he wheezed. "What's she doing here?"

Hannah said, "This is Pokey. She lives with me. You'll have to get used to it."

He made a wide circle and she grinned when he passed. Hannah stayed on the back porch while he was in the bathroom (so he wouldn't run away, Pokey guessed), and when they came back Pokey grinned again, wide and toothy.

He stopped. "Who are you?"

"I'm just a kid."

"Why are you bothering me?"

"I'm not. I . . . wanted to help."

He peered at her closely and said, "Huhhh."

Hannah said, "It's early. We'll sit with you awhile."

Ross hesitated. "But . . ."

"Don't worry. You're safe here."

He froze. "Even *you* say it."

"Say what?"

"You are safe here."

"Oh." Hannah thought for a minute, then told him, "Those words are on the television all the time. They float in your head, like song lyrics used to."

Ross was suspicious of Hannah now. He drew away from her guiding hands, climbed into bed and, with the sheet pulled up for protection, said, "I can't believe you're part of it."

"Part of what?"

"The . . . what I . . ." He was pale and huge-eyed. "What I saw."

"I don't know what you saw, but I'm not."

"I . . . can't talk about it."

"You don't have to. Ross, I—" Hannah sat on the edge of her easy chair. "I'm an old woman. I've lived through a terrible time. Done all I could for my friends, neighbors, strangers. I have lived alone until recently." She didn't glance at Pokey. "All I know is Harpers Ferry. I do not understand what you think I am 'part of.' "

"Harpers Ferry? Is that where we are?"

"Yes. Across two rivers into West Virginia."

"I was on my way to Washington. How . . . how far?"

"Sixty-five miles."

Ross lay still, his eyes on the end of the bed. Pokey had taken a place on a low trunk near the open window. Hannah had begun to knit, with a pleasant, easy expression that asked no questions, but waited.

Finally Ross spoke. "I'm going to Washington because . . . well, I heard rumors and I guess they're true. You mentioned TV, you have electricity. Do those things come from Washington?" Hannah nodded. "Then it's

70

far ahead. Everywhere else, all I've seen is . . . pockets of people trying to get by, barely managing. In some places . . . do you know about Chicago?"

Pokey and the old woman shook their heads.

"I met this guy on the road. He said, 'Chicago is abandoned.' All those big buildings with all the people. The survivors couldn't cope. They just moved out, left the city to the dead. No one goes there. I stayed well to the south."

Pokey said, "In Washington they hauled away the dead."

"All of them?" She nodded. "Amazing."

Pokey couldn't hold back anymore; the questions burst out. "How did you get here? Nobody travels now. How could you do it?"

"I drove."

"Drove? Do you know how? Are you old enough?"

"I turned sixteen a month ago," he announced with his chin up. "Of course I know how." He stared at Pokey, suspicious again. "Why do you ask so many questions?"

"I . . ." Pokey twisted her fingers.

"Don't mind her," Hannah told him. "It's her nature."

Ross squinted uncertainly and Pokey said, "Sorry."

"Besides," said Hannah, "why wouldn't we be curious? You appear in our midst like an apparition with tales of far away." Ross smiled and Hannah went on, winning him. "How did you learn to drive?"

"Well, Tostado—after I got out of the hospital—we kind of taught each other."

He took a sip of water and Hannah said, "If you feel up to it, start at the beginning."

Happy to talk, he began, "I was in the hospital when the cloud came, in traction because I'd broken my leg in a skiing accident. End-of-the-season. I got out of bed, scooted around in a wheelchair with my leg sticking out.

Did what I could for people, you know. Ended up down in the boiler room with this engineer named Hank. He'd been in Vietnam. Boy, he knew his stuff."

"What kind of stuff?" asked Hannah.

"Electrical." Ross sounded proud. "He taught me everything he knew and we kept the hospital going, even when the city power went out. 'Spit and chewing gum,' Hank used to say, 'will work wonders if you've got some basic equipment.' The hospital had auxiliary generators and we moved circuits for the operating rooms, delivery rooms, elevators . . ." He looked straight ahead. "While we waited to get sick."

"But you didn't," Hannah murmured.

"No. After a while, Hank went off, said he was gonna go live in the mountains, up near Silver Plume. I . . . left, too, there wasn't anybody much sick anymore. Went out and met up with Tostado and the guys."

"Who?" said Hannah. "Tostado is a name?"

"Yep. He changed it. Now he's Tostado Grande. Why not? There's nobody keeping records."

Hannah shook her head. "Maybe you shouldn't talk. Over-excited."

"No, I'm fine." He was wound up, anxious to go on. "We taught each other to drive. We couldn't get at gas, but there were plenty of cars in running order every- where. Me and Tostado and the guys figured out how to jump them, it's easy, and we drove every car in Den- ver, I bet. Drove 'em all, right through buildings, off bridges, into windows. Because we were mad. I mean, how could this happen?" He sat up, glaring angrily from Pokey to Hannah. Then dropped back onto the pillows and went on. "After a few months the gang sort of drifted apart. Most of the cars in Denver were out of gas, what else was there to do? It's not so much fun to get in trouble if nobody cares. We weren't into fires . . ."

Pokey shivered. There had been fires where she lived in Arlington. She leaned in the window, looking out. Dark was falling. There were no sounds, no lights. Nothing.

Hannah dropped a stitch and muttered to herself, picking it up.

Ross continued. "So I left the guys, went back home. My folks had a big old house and some land outside of town. They called it a ranch but it wasn't really. I hadn't been back since . . . since." Pokey didn't look at him, his voice cracked. "Anyway. The caretaker was still there. He was an old Indian guy named Joe Silver, and he'd worked on the place for about a hundred years. It was always more his than anybody's. He was sleeping in my dad's bed, smoking his pipes. Sad as an old cactus. I stayed with him for a few weeks and one afternoon I said, 'Come on, Joe. I'll take you for a ride.' " Ross grinned in remembrance.

"Yes?" said Hannah.

"The car I picked out had something wrong with its gas gauge. We ran out about ten miles east of Denver. In the desert. On the long walk back, Joe told me about people in the Depression who'd picked the locks on gas pumps. I said, 'Really? There's plenty of gas, must be thousands of stations with full tanks in the ground. If I could get at it, I could go anywhere.' All he said, was, 'Hmm.' I was nearly jumping out of my skin with excitement but I knew better than to keep on asking. Old Joe would clam up on me. He didn't like to be pushed. What he did was measure me with those cool dark eyes and say 'Let me think.'

"So we walked, and after about five miles he stopped and said, 'Well, it's the same old sky. Maybe some things work the same.' At the house he tinkered and fiddled in his workshop until he made it: a long, skinny piece of metal, zigzagged on one side and smooth on the other." He patted his chest and legs. "Give it back."

"Your clothes are on the chair," Hannah said with great dignity. "Pocket goods by the bed."

Pokey noticed the small collection for the first time: several keys, a thin spiky thing, two smashed candy bars, and a whistle. Ross picked up the slender spike. "It wasn't quite that easy. Gas pumps work by electricity now. But I went up in the mountains near Silver Plume, looked until I found Hank. He knew what to do. Drove me to an old Air Force depot and got me a real fine little generator. And here I am."

"You didn't come in a car," said Hannah.

"No. I stopped in Iowa for a while. There was this woman, Alice Bortman, and a bunch of kids living on what used to be a beef-cattle spread. I got sick there—everybody had colds and sore throats—and I thought I was better, but after Indiana I felt sort of woozy and the roads got complicated and I . . . in Ohio I stopped . . ."

He frowned and put a hand to his head. His cheeks were pink, his eyes glittery.

"You're tired, boy," said Hannah gently.

"Call me Ross, will you?"

"Ross. Time for your medicine." She went to get it. Pokey gazed out the window. There was a sound in the bushes, but nothing moved.

Ross said, "Is somebody out there?"

Pokey wasn't sure but she said, "No," and held her breath. Ross groaned and lay back as if sleeping. Pokey stayed out of sight of the dark window until Hannah came back with the medicine and a tall glass of water. "I think someone's out there," she whispered.

Hannah glanced at the window. "Humh."

"Could it be Skip Clinton?"

"No. Skip doesn't come quietly. Makes enough noise to wake the dead."

Ross opened his eyes. "What's that? Somebody?"

"No. Probably the cat. She stalks at night." Hannah changed the subject. "You say you understand electricity, bo—, Ross?"

"You bet. I could wire a whole town. Did wire part of Iowa for Alice Bortman. That's why I'm going to Washington."

"You should tell John McQuarter. He takes care of our electricity, in private, you might say. I help him."

Ross swallowed his penicillin, took a long drink of water, then said with a yawn, "Harpers Ferry. I learned about that in school."

"Yes?" said Hannah.

"I know: 'The shot heard round the world.'"

Pokey shook her head.

"No? Let me think." His glass tilted sideways. "Oh, now I know." He sang with big round vowels, "'John Brown's body' . . ."

Hannah smiled. "You're right. But that was long ago. Now it's different. There are no raiders here. Just a sick boy and two peculiar womenfolk. And it's time for bed."

Pokey liked being one of the "peculiar womenfolk," especially since Ross, who was four years older, had been called a boy. Grinning secretly, she said good night and went upstairs.

In bed, she noticed the dark square of the window.

There was no curtain or shade and she thought, *What if somebody's out there, looking in?*

She switched off the lamp. The window was near the top branches of a maple tree, far too high for anyone to see in. Down in the yard nothing moved. The night was more peaceful than night had seemed for a long time. She stayed, watching the outline of hills, listening to the sound of the rivers, until she heard Hannah open the door at the bottom of the stairs. A shaft of light came up.

Quickly, she slipped into bed and closed her eyes.

Hannah straightened the covers, then leaned over Pokey with her arms outstretched.

"All these children," she whispered. "Lord help me."

In the morning John McQuarter shook Pokey's shoulder. When she opened her eyes he said, "Come on. I need your help."

"Huh?"

"You heard me."

In the kitchen, Hannah whispered, "Morning. Sh-hh, get dressed." Pokey did, quickly, in the bathroom, and when she came out Hannah and John gestured, *Come on*, and led her to the porch.

Hannah spoke softly. "Ross had bad dreams all night. Poor thing. I can't leave him."

"Bah," said John. "We all have bad dreams."

"Not me," said Pokey.

"Pokey," said Hannah, "there's an emergency. Will you go with John to the electric plant down on the Potomac?"

"They're cutting off our power," John added.

"Already?" Pokey asked. "How do you know? The lights are on."

76

"I have a digital clock radio. There's no broadcasting but it responds to interference. It started flashing at five A.M."

Pokey wasn't wide awake enough to say so, but she understood. She'd had one of those radios herself, back in the old days, and she'd often fallen asleep to the Top Forty Countdown. During thunderstorms, if the power went off for even a minute, the clock would go crazy: forget the time, forget its alarm functions, blink on and off.

"So come on. It's a small readjustment but I need your help." He started down the steps.

She didn't follow. "I . . ."

He paused. "What's the matter?"

"You . . ."

"Go on," Hannah urged. "Tell him."

Encouraged, Pokey blurted, "You wanted me to go away. I'm not gonna . . . go with you."

John McQuarter reclimbed the stairs. "Now, see here. Hannah, reason with her."

Hannah looked every bit as stubborn as Pokey. "No. You explain yourself, John."

"All right." Persuasive and confident, he began, "That was yesterday. All I saw was . . . a problem. More trouble. But I was outvoted. Hannah wants you to stay. *You* want to. Now there's a boy. OK, fine. Stay. Let's get on with it." He reached out to shake her hand.

Pokey scowled.

"Don't you know about politics? If a vote goes against me, I say, 'OK.' Accept it, work with those people on the next thing. It's nothing personal."

Pokey thought, *It seems personal to me*, but Hannah said, "Go on. We need you. It's all right." So Pokey slid out her hand, carefully keeping it as limp as a rag.

77

"Fine." The congressman shook firmly. "Now, hurry. There's no time to lose."

Hannah patted Pokey's arm. "Be careful."

They trailed down the path between houses to the wooden stairs. *He's heading for the railroad station. If he tries to take me there, I'll run . . .*

Turning left at the dirt road, away from the station, he slowed to let her catch up. "Beautiful morning, isn't it?"

Pokey wasn't about to be tricked into pleasantries. "Ross says most places don't have electricity. They don't even make it anymore."

"Yes. I believe that's true."

"We always had it where I was. Sometimes it was a little pale but it hardly ever went out."

"Where were you?"

"In Arlington."

"Ah, near the Pentagon. Washington has rather re-markable resources. We kept it going. Used our advanced technology to solve new problems."

"Who's we?"

"A bunch of us—government workers, army people, city people. We were living in the Capital, actually at the State Department building, running things, coping with problems . . ." They were out of town. Up ahead the road rose to meet the railroad track. John frowned and asked, "Say, were you out on your own when the heat-sensitive TV's came on?"

"I didn't like it."

"It was a remarkable achievement. We had a dispersed population, out of communication, frightened. We needed to reach them. . . . You say you didn't like it?"

"Scared me." The set had come on without warning,

with no picture, just sound: "Hello. This is an experiment in heat-sensitive transmission. Stay tuned. Stay nearby. Instructions will follow." She shivered, the voice was still so clear. "I didn't know how it found me."

"The idea came from two engineers who'd worked for a subcontractor for DOD—"

"What's that?"

"Department of Defense. They'd been perfecting technology for heat-seeking weapons tied to electronic receivers. It was a new idea to use that capability to find sources of heat, 96 to 104 degrees Fahrenheit, in masses of forty pounds or more. In other words, people near television sets—"

"Or big dogs. There was this sheep dog I fed sometimes. It roamed around and started the TV's talking in rooms I knew were empty. I'd have to sneak up and see why . . ."

"We couldn't help that."

"It was spooky. I hated it."

When the messages started coming (after weeks of "Stay tuned"), they were stern, bossy, confusing. She ignored them, lived on cold canned goods from the other apartments, and stayed far from the set, watching out the dining room window. Sometimes she saw the sheep dog, a huddled figure, a trail of smoke. The stoplight on the corner blinked red, yellow, green.

That was all.

He said, "But you knew what to do, when you were ready."

"I guess."

Across the railroad track, an old stone building straddled the riverbank. A dam stretched behind it, with water flowing over in a constant roar. Pokey realized she'd been hearing the sound of water, louder and louder, and a steady throb of machinery as well. Wires drooped from reinforced holes high in the wall, traveled a short distance to gray columns in a fenced-in yard marked DANGER, HIGH VOLTAGE, then marched across the river and up the mountain, heading for the city.

In the powerhouse, the floor shook. Two large generators vibrated, spinning inside. "Careful," her companion warned as they skirted the machines. Pokey looked into a steep shaft and saw, far below, the top of a turbine. A deafening hum surrounded her. She read his lips: "This way."

They went up an iron stairway to a small closed-in balcony above the river.

It was quieter. Across one wall ranged a row of gray metal boxes. One of them had a fluorescent pink ribbon tied to its handle. "That's Skip's circuit breaker. He needs a bow so he'll remember which one is his. He doesn't much like electricity." John bent to peer behind some stacked lumber at another dusty-looking breaker. "Ah, you see?"

The handle stood partway between ON and OFF.

"It's going off," she said.

"Yes." He took a deep breath. "All right. Here's the story."

He looked so serious that Pokey got worried.

"The computer at headquarters is programmed to search out all empty houses and unauthorized drawing of—"

"But why? Empty houses don't use electricity."

"Sure they do. For refrigerators, clocks, water heaters,

anything that's still plugged in and running. That random use adds up."

"*We're* not random use. We're people."

"But not authorized. Headquarters found us again last night. They began directing surges through the line to cut off our power."

Pokey swallowed. "It's my fault, you know."

"How's that?"

"The person at headquarters told Skip Clinton he was putting an extra query into the files by Harpers Ferry. Because of me."

John smiled. "Relax. They've tried to knock us out of the system plenty of times. You're not entirely responsible."

"Hmm." She reached out to the breaker. "So what do we do? Push this thing up?"

"Careful! No!"

Pokey jerked back as if struck.

"You might get a shock. I have to adjust the splice connection first. That's why it's a . . . two-man job."

He opened a dirty, mesh-covered window. Outside, on thin local-service wires, were two orange balls. Pointing to them, he explained, "You see, these are part of the new technology. Electricity is drawn off to run lights here in this building, and a line runs to Skip, for his station, the park, and the lower town. *His* power passes perfectly through an orange ball and isn't questioned. *Ours*—"

"The other one is ours?"

"Yes. When I left Washington I chose Harpers Ferry because of this hydroelectric plant. And I brought along my own private splicing ball because I knew how my colleagues planned to use them. Only . . . I can't get it adjusted right. Sometimes the searches bump an edge and find us."

"And try to shut off your lights?"

"And refrigerators, heaters, televisions. That means contact, news. Mine, then Hannah's, the Watson sisters', other people living in the next town and beyond. Once our power is gone, we won't be able to get it back. The loss will creep inward, to Brunswick, then Point of Rocks." His eyes flashed, hard as steel. "We should not be compelled to move into the city. Or to live like medievals out here, scratching together firewood, lugging water. Things have been hard enough. It's not fair."

He's not such a cool politician about everything, Pokey thought, liking him better. "What do I do?"

He moved the lumber. "Stand here. When I tell you, hold the lever. When you feel a . . . tingling, push up."

"Tingling?" Her voice quivered. She remembered the sign outside: DANGER, HIGH—"V-voltage?" *Suppose he just wants to kill me?*

He hesitated. "You'll feel more than a tingling. It's a surge of current. You'll have to be very brave."

"Will it hurt me?"

"No. I'll be holding it back."

"You'll feel the current, too?"

"Yes."

She wasn't really courageous; she believed him, and climbed onto the boards. "Let's go."

He straddled the window ledge and leaned out of sight. "Now. Let me know when you've got it."

She approached the breaker, touched the metal. It was cool, stiff, silent. She waited, telling herself, *This isn't so bad*. Then felt, around knee level, a faint rumbling. She let go, thinking something was wrong with the turbines downstairs. The lever moved an inch toward OFF.

Oh, no. I missed it.

When the next surge came she closed her eyes. It touched her belly, her joints; then in a sudden easing, the handle loosened. She pushed it upward. *I don't like this.*

The second surge was no worse. On the third she realized she could open her eyes and almost breathe while it was happening. The fourth hardly touched the breaker and passed on. The lever was at the top.

She let go gingerly and called, "Done!" then wobbled and sank to the floor.

John McQuarter climbed back through the window. "Are you all right? Rest a minute."

Pokey pulled herself together. "I'm fine. Let's get out of here."

As they walked, John McQuarter shepherded her, almost touching her elbow and shoulder blades. Pokey hugged herself. The thought of Hannah, standing on those boards, her long fingers trembling, was upsetting. "Do you have to do that often? With Hannah?"

"More and more. Headquarters keeps at it. The surges come back. I can't get the splice right."

Pokey said, "I don't like it."

"Me neither."

"Hey, you know what? Ross understands electricity. He said so. May be he could fix it."

McQuarter frowned. "So I heard. But this is far more complicated."

Pokey remembered the rustling outside Hannah's window. "Was that you last night? Listening?"

He ducked his head in embarrassment, then drew up to full height. "You're too curious," he snapped, walking faster.

"Hey, wait up. I—"

They were near the station and John McQuarter suddenly barked, "Hide! Quick!" and shoved her toward the bushes.

Pokey dove and froze.

"Morning, Skip," John called, leaping up the embankment to the parking lot. "Whatcha doing?"

"Oh, trouble, more trouble, always trouble," grumbled the stationmaster. "Where've you been?"

"Checking the hydroelectric plant. I pulled some debris from one of the intake bays. You ought to check them more often."

"I can't do everything."

"No."

"I've got news for you." Skip Clinton's voice was unhappy. "Bad news."

"Oh?"

"Got new orders. Because of what happened here the other day—lost kids, drownded kids—I've gotta beef up security here in the park."

"That's a bother. How?" Sympathy dripped from John's tone.

"And I'm to get you folks to move away."

"What?"

"They've said it before. This time they really mean it. 'You have too much population,' they say. I'm to find out how you get your electric power and shut it off. You, Hannah, everyone."

"Skip, you know where I just was?" The only answer was silence. "You know you hate to go there. You can't do everything yourself. Be sensible. Could you get Hannah to leave peacefully?" He chuckled. "I'd like to see you try getting the Watsons to do anything they don't want to do."

"Force."

84

"Then you'd be here alone. You wouldn't have me to help you. You know how much help *they* send. What would you do?"

"You could stay! As my assistant."

"No. I'll do what I can, but I will not be your"—he spat it out—"assistant."

"I don't know why you think you can always order me around. I'm the stationmaster here." He sounded petulant.

John McQuarter didn't answer him directly. "What's this you're working on?"

"Bit of loose track. There's another train coming through tomorrow. You know, there's no work crews anymore. They expect me to fix everything."

"I'll help you. Hand me the sledgehammer. You say another train?"

"Yep. In the morning. Clearing out the city, I understand."

Metal hit metal with a resounding ring, *Twing, twank.* Then John McQuarter said, "This is hard work. Why don't we do it later? I could use a cup of coffee."

"With me? You want to have coffee with me? Great! Come on."

Pokey heard the door slam. She thought, *He's getting Skip away so I can escape* . . . She climbed out of the bushes, rubbing her arm where he had pushed her. *He sure did jump to save me.*

Her smile lay frozen when she remembered, *Another train? Full of kids? So soon?*

CHAPTER SEVEN
Ohio State

 "A REAL HYDROELECTRIC PLANT?" Ross asked when she got back. "In operation?"

"Yes. Everything quivers and shakes. It's got high voltage."

"I want to see it."

Hannah turned from the stove where she was stirring a pot of oatmeal. "You leave it alone. At least, until you're better." She gave him an appraising glance. He was rosy-cheeked and tousled, with big circles under his eyes. "Till *I* say you're better. Pokey? You hungry?"

"I was, but . . ." She looked down at the clothes she'd thrown on for the third straight day. "Could I have a bath first?"

"Certainly."

The tub stood on high claw feet. Pokey washed her hair, feet, knees, all over everywhere twice. That done, she slid down and let her hair float out, keeping only her nose out of the water, submerging and rising slowly like a lazy walrus.

She put on a new outfit: clean black socks; Lucy's daughter's striped underwear; a soft, old-lady-pink vest; the man's pale collarless shirt and gray pants, held up with the stretchy gold belt. Last of all, she tied the silk scarf around her neck.

Drying her hair with a towel, she ruffled it with both hands and grinned at her reflection.

When she came out, Ross whistled and Hannah turned to her. "Those are Sam's clothes."

"I know," said Pokey. "I was wondering about Sam."

"I told you, he was my husband. Died in the Second War. Long ago."

"I thought you were *Miss* Hannah."

" 'Miss' by custom, not fact."

"Oh. Is it all right if I wear them?"

"He wouldn't mind. They become you."

Pokey snuck a look at Ross and blushed. She hadn't changed her clothes or washed her hair for his benefit. But his response was gratifying.

Pokey waited until late morning to say what was on her mind. They were sitting on the porch, with sun flooding the yard, the treetops, the mountain.

"Skip Clinton . . . says there's another train coming tomorrow."

Hannah stopped rocking.

Ross said, "What do you mean?"

"Like the one I came on. Out from the city."

"I don't understand." He swung his feet down from the glider, his blanket slipping. "Haven't you always lived here? Upstairs?"

"Since the day before yesterday. I was on that train, the one you rode. When it was going the other way." Pokey felt breathless, the unspoken crowding her mind. She didn't want to upset him again, but she had to go on. "A lot of kids I knew were on it, too. They went to Ohio."

"No. Hannah?"

"Yes. She escaped from the train. From inside it."

Ross squeezed his arms across his chest, staring at

Pokey as if she was from another world. "You're one of those kids."

She nodded.

"And the words you said to me . . ."

"Yes?"

"You're lucky you got out of there."

Pokey held very still. "I know."

"I better tell you," he whispered, moving his gaze to the porch rail. "I . . . I've kind of lost track of time."

Hannah said, "You arrived here yesterday."

"Yes, well." He shuddered. "Then it was the night before last. I'd been driving a long time and I was tired and lost. It was . . . Ohio somewhere. You . . . don't know how dark and strange it is at night now, out on the highway."

Pokey and Hannah nodded.

"I guess I was sick even then. I know I was too tired to go on. I pulled off the road and went to sleep in the front seat of my pickup truck. All of a sudden, *whoosh*, something barreled by. Woke me with such a jolt, I jumped and hit my head. My heart was beating so fast it was like the ground was still shaking. Then another one came: *swoosh*! It was a big bus, going lickety-split after the first one."

"A bus?" Pokey asked.

"That's what I thought, 'Buses?' I sat up, started the engine. Didn't put on my headlights. I . . . I don't know why. There was something too . . . purposeful about the buses. Nobody acts like that anymore."

Hannah frowned. "You can smell it."

"Then another one came. I eased out onto the highway after it.

"Driving, I asked myself, 'What are you doing?' but I didn't stop. I was wide awake and interested. Here were people, going somewhere, fast. They went south for about fifty miles and I followed, keeping their bobbing red lights in sight. We reached a city, Columbus, left the Interstate, zigzagged around, and pretty soon we passed through an arch and were on the campus of . . . Ohio State University. The buses parked. I stopped about half a block away, cut the engine, opened the passenger door, and ran for the shadows."

Muscles along the insides of Pokey's arms were trembling. She squeezed her elbows tight to her sides and didn't take her eyes off Ross.

"I snuck closer and saw kids. They got off the buses and lined up by a building across the street. The doors were closed; everybody just stood there, with big spotlights shining down from the roof and the bus lights on them from behind. They didn't whisper or giggle or even move around much."

"I know them," Pokey murmured.

"Out of nowhere a car screeched up. 'Hi there, Tom, everybody,' a man called. 'Took you long enough. I went home for some shuteye.' He was wearing bright-red pajama tops, and bottoms, too, they stuck out under his pants. 'Somebody here bring that pickup?' he hollered, pointing at my truck. 'No,' one of the grown-ups answered. 'Come on.' The new guy scratched his head, trotted back, peered in, and took out the keys. (They were there, of course, dumb me.) He stuck them in his pocket, muttering to himself, 'Hmmm. This truck here before? Dunno. . . . Don't think so.' One of the women called, 'Hurry up. You've kept us waiting long enough.' 'Coming,' the man said. As he walked, he kept turning around, searching the shadows. I didn't wait. I ducked into the nearest building.

"It was a dormitory. Off the entrance there were long

halls with soft lights burning . . . and cots. Rows of cots with kids lying on them, sleeping. I rushed to the far end, waited near a stairway to see if anyone was chasing me. But they weren't. Then I . . . heard a voice. It was low and soothing, saying the words you said to me—"

" 'Remember,' " Pokey whispered. " 'We are safe here. All things' . . ."

"Yes. So soft you could barely hear them, repeating over and over. While the kids . . ."

"Yes," Hannah urged. "Go on."

"Each one was so quiet. Every sheet was draped across, perfectly smooth. They were breathing; when I looked close I could see each mound move a little. But it wasn't natural sleep. It was kind of . . . suspension."

"We slept in the halls in Washington." Pokey's voice was loud. "But people snored, sleepwalked. Cried. The beds were a mess."

"Not these. You could tell, they'd be just like that in the morning. I took the stairway up to the second floor. It was worse, darker. Another endless corridor with the same recorded voice. More cots. But these, each one had an . . . intravenous bag hanging above the bed, with liquid dripping into tubes, into needles strapped onto their hands, then . . . it must have gone into veins. Nobody moved . . . they barely breathed. I backed up. All I wanted was a way out.

"I knew the live, waked-up people were the ones to be afraid of, but the kids scared me more. I slipped down another hall, found a side door. Sleeping on a cot nearby was a guy about my age. He stirred when I passed and went, 'Uhhhh.' I knelt beside him. 'Hey, man,' I said, 'Wake up.' His eyes fluttered open, and he looked sort of right through me and said, 'Hey, man,' and closed his eyes. I said, 'Wake up. I've got a car. Come on, let's get out of here.' "

Ross was silent a long minute. "I would have liked to get just one guy out of there. Only one. But he wouldn't budge. Kind of smiled. He was drugged, not sleeping. His arm felt like rubber where I pulled it. There was a sore on his elbow. I . . . had to leave him. When I looked back, the voice had stopped, but not one of them had moved."

Restless, Pokey stood and paced from one end of the porch to the other, then returned and leaned against the rail to listen again.

Hannah said gently, "Then what?"

"I crept around the building to where I could see what was going on. Across the way, the line of kids was much shorter; most of them were already inside. I couldn't see what was happening in there, but I could imagine. My truck . . . might as well have been a thousand miles away. There were people around. I didn't have the keys. They'd get me before I could jump it."

He kept his eyes downcast, as if he was ashamed. "I wanted to yell, 'Hey, you. Whadda you think you're doing? Let those kids go!' But I didn't. I bit my hand and kept quiet.

"When they were all processed, the older people came out and stood talking. 'We'll be back in Washington well before noon,' a woman said. I started grinning: 'That's where I'm heading.' I crossed my fingers, kept my head down, and slipped onto a bus. Halfway to the rear, I crouched on the floor between seats.

"The man Tom got on my bus and started the motor, then leaned out the window to talk to the guy in charge. I guess they were brothers because he said, 'How's Mom?

Tell her I'll try to stop next time. We're awful busy right now.' Somebody else tooted a horn, and Tom hollered, 'Hold on!' then asked, 'You sure you don't need more help? Got a lot of kids here.'

"The fellow in the red pajamas took a minute, then said, 'Maybe. The new hibernation drug works good. We can make big supplies of it right here in the lab. But . . . even so we have to let up sometimes. Rouse them, feed 'em cereal. Yecch.' He coughed. 'Clean 'em up. Yes, I can use help.' 'OK,' Tom promised and his brother went on. 'When you want 'em back, we're gonna have to work on muscles.' He sounded worried. 'They do get flabby.' "

That would be me. Pokey felt sick to her stomach. *Right . . . there.*

"I should have killed them. Done anything to stop it. But I . . . couldn't." He looked anxiously at Hannah.

Her voice was low. "Of course not. You did exactly right."

"One swat with Mr. P.J.'s needle and I'd be a goner, too. But . . . now all I think about is those kids. It's like they followed me."

I'm safe. Thank goodness. Pokey put her face in her hands. *But the others—*

"I figured we'd ride the bus a long time—all the way to Washington. But pretty soon we stopped at an old railroad siding. Not even a station, no town in sight. They parked the buses in a row and got out, three women and a man. Gave the keys to the big lady—"

"Matron."

"Who dropped them in her purse. A train was waiting. 'Hi, there,' the engineer called. 'Ready? I got 'er turned around.' They headed for the train and I wondered what to do. I could have stayed and jumped one of the buses, but I knew it would only run out of gas. I didn't have my generator. It was in my pickup. I—" He bit a fingernail. "I think I should go back for it."

"No," said Hannah.

"Anyway, the train started rolling, and I ran and climbed on top. It swayed a lot; there wasn't much to hang on to. I grabbed the top rung of a ladder and held that and the center ridge. The train went for hours, slippery—" His hands were clenched like they had been at first, raw and red. "Boy, was it slippery.

"It got to be daylight. The wind was so loud, the sky so bright. I tried not to think about the kids. I just rode away with my head banging and my throat shut, still hearing those words."

You were brave, Pokey thought, and went to sit beside him again.

"When the train stopped—I suppose I'd been sort of sleeping—I reared up and saw a big tunnel ahead, a river, a town. A parking lot full of cars. I remember thinking, 'I don't like this. I have to get away.'" He paused. "I'd heard that people were getting things going in Washington. It sounded like a place that was far ahead. But . . . nobody ever said there was stuff like this going on." He pleaded, "Pokey, you were there. Tell me, *why?*"

"I . . . I don't know. We weren't supposed to think about problems." There were some things she knew. Last winter everyone had been cold and hungry. The summer before, new germ strains had made countless people fall ill. The water was suspected, and the food. Rumors flew: new epidemics; survivors from the north (like Boston) or overseas, massed to attack; danger and safety, twisted.

93

Haltingly, she told what she could, then said, "Matron and the others, they say they'll take care of the worry. They say all things are temporary. They work hard and they tell us we're safe, but inside . . . we're all scared. Them, too." Remembering the obedient lines of children who took comfort from being close to one another, she fell silent and studied the uneven boards on the porch deck, brown and wavy.

Hannah spoke. "As if what happened wasn't enough . . . What are these people thinking? Hauling children away, drugging them. So what if they get things started? They're," her hands clenched, "dead wrong."

Pokey didn't have any answers. She wished she could close her eyes to everything.

Hannah gazed at the distant hill. "Girl, fetch my harmonica."

"Wh-where is it?"

"Living room. On the mantel."

Pokey found it. It was small and silver, comfortable in her hand. She carried the instrument to Hannah and sat on the top step, her arms wrapped around her knees.

Hannah rocked a while before beginning to play: one long, soft-held note, like crying.

Ross leaned back, his body tight, his eyes closed. The thread of music increased, simply expressing pain. Pokey couldn't stand it. She stumbled to her feet.

"I'm going for a walk."

The playing stopped. "Where?"

"There's more town, isn't there? Up beyond you? I haven't seen it." Hannah frowned. Pokey took a step into the yard. "I'll be OK. It's safe, isn't it?"

Reluctantly, Hannah nodded. "Skip doesn't go there. But you . . . are you all right?"

"Yes. Sure."

94

"Be careful. Don't stay long."

"I won't." Ross sat up as if to follow, then sank back at a firm shake of Hannah's head.

The woman said, "Take the high fork. You'll go by Lucy's."

"OK."

She walked fast so she wouldn't hear the harmonica again, telling herself, *Don't worry. You can think about everything later. Don't worry . . .*

It wasn't easy. The nightmare image of the old familiar rows of cots, transformed to what Ross had seen, was too possible, too real. She broke into a run, her eyes on tree trunks, mentally counting them one-two-three. The road curved upward and opened onto a wide residential street.

The second house on the right had a well-tended garden inside a picket fence. *That's Lucy's house, I bet. Hannah takes care of it.*

Slowing down, she jogged on until she was out of breath. She paused at another fence, looking down into a tangled garden with daffodils pushing up through two years' worth of weeds. *How quiet it is. And nobody around . . .*

There was a playground behind an old school, with swings. She'd been a champion swinger in the third grade, and she ran to them. Pumped until she was flying high, then stretched out her legs, leaned way back and coasted, with wind singing in her ears. She told herself, *It's all right. You are safe here . . .*

When she'd had enough she swung high, then leaped, scraping her knees on the gravel.

Winding around, she crossed Main Street, then climbed a steep block to another road, high above the river. *Aren't those power lines? That's the Potomac.*

There were no sidewalks, so she walked in the middle

of the street, watching the river appear and disappear between houses, until a strange voice called, "Yoo-hoo!"

She stopped, dumbfounded.

"Yoo-hoo! Girl! Hello there!" It was a woman, grinning from under a big straw hat, waving a pair of gardening clippers. She was standing near some bushes in front of a sleek new house that teetered on the edge of a cliff.

"Hi," Pokey answered, wondering, *Who in the world . . . ?*

"Wait a minute," the woman hissed, turning to yell, "Sissy! Come out. Here she is."

Pokey just stood, staring.

"Aren't you the girl who's staying with Miss Hannah? Have you come to tea?"

"N-n-no," Pokey stuttered. "Not me."

"Oh. Too bad. Sissy!" Pokey glanced toward the house and saw a woman in the doorway, an apron held to her mouth. She waved. This one wore no hat but aside from that seemed very like the other: a little plumper, with frizzy gray curls, pink cheeks, and a flowered dress.

Pokey grinned. These must be the Watson sisters. "Are you Miss Watson?"

The lady took a few quick swipes at an imaginary vine, *snip, snip,* in Pokey's direction. "Yes. Miss Maude Watson. That's Sissy." She pointed with the clippers and confided, "She's younger than I. Only fifty-three. And odd."

"Oh." *You're pretty odd yourself.* "How'd you know about me staying with Hannah?"

"Saw you with her. But I haven't seen Miss Hannah out walking lately." She emphasized the "Miss" as if scolding Pokey for using Hannah's first name. "Is she unwell?"

"No. She's been busy, you know, with the boy."

"A boy!" Miss Watson shouted with glee. "Is there a boy, too? Is he white?"

"Ross? Yes."

"Sissy!" she bellowed. "There's a boy, too!"

"Please be quiet," Pokey begged. "We're not supposed to be here. It's a secret."

"A secret?" Miss Watson looked horrified. "You mean we're supposed to report you?"

"What? No!!"

The woman squinted suspiciously. "Does John McQuarter know you're here?"

"Yes! Yes, he does. I helped him this morning."

"And Mr. Skip Clinton?"

"N-no."

"Well, I don't know," said Miss Watson, straightening her hat and squaring her shoulders. "We don't want anything irregular happening in Harpers Ferry."

"Oh, please, you can't tell. We . . ." Pokey couldn't begin to explain. "Please . . ."

The younger Miss Watson approached and tugged at her sister's sleeve. She glanced at Pokey, smiled briefly, and murmured, "We haven't been introduced."

"Ah-hh, Pokey. Pokey Hughes."

"How do you do?" She turned, businesslike, to her sister. "Now, Maude, come in the house. I'll fix you a nice toddy. That Mr. Clinton was very rude the last time we talked to him, don't you remember? Don't worry, dear. I'm sure if Miss Hannah wants children, it's up to her." She gestured at Pokey, an abrupt flap of the hand that said, *Go away!* and drew her sister toward the house.

"Oh, Sissy, do you think so? Do you think it's all right? I don't want trouble."

Miss Sissy Watson looked back from the doorway and winked at Pokey. "One of them keeps children, the other keeps chickens. We're lucky we have each other." She slammed the door.

Pokey stared at the silent house. Taking a few steps backward, she noticed in the side yard several large bird feeders, platforms really, spread full of nuts and seeds. *Birds? Boy, I'd love to see one.* A curtain twitched; the Watsons were watching.

Pokey trailed toward Hannah's, not ready to return, slowing until she stopped in the middle of the road, stuck.

Ross's story, and all she remembered of cots and corridors, came flooding back. She couldn't stop memory, or hide.

They wanted to get rid of us. We were too much trouble— no matter how good we were! It isn't fair!

She was angry and hot, breathing fast. *All those kids . . . and Miss Vanderpugh knew! I hate her, I hate them all.*

The dusty street shimmered as Pokey fought back tears.

The Children's Concern: "We take care of the worry." Ha! They don't. They make mistakes. I should laugh instead of cry. . . .

She didn't move until a tall, familiar figure came marching toward her. "Hannah!"

"Came to find you." The woman put her hands on her hips. She was breathing hard, but through her nose as if pretending not to.

"You're out of breath."

"I am not. Ready to come back?"

"Oh, Hannah. How could they?"

"Your Children's Concerners? They are wrong." She

98

tucked Pokey's hand into the crook of her arm and started walking.

Pokey squeezed Hannah's arm and lengthened her stride. "I . . . met the Watsons."

"Oh?"

"Yes. They . . . are they always like that?"

Hannah slowed down, flicked a smile back toward the sisters' house. "Miss Maude and Sissy Watson were never what you'd call, ah . . . usual. They used to lead wildlife tours, bird-watching safaris. Inherited the business from their father. During the sickness—" She patted Pokey's hand and chuckled. "It's funny how people surprise you. I'd have thought they'd stay in the house, twitch and fidget. And die for sure. But they didn't. They came out every day, worked hard, never flagging. They were a lesson to me."

And you to them, I bet. "They manage there, the two of them?"

"We help each other. We all manage. They've lived here for years, though not always in that house."

"Oh." There was one more thing about the Watsons. "They didn't tell Skip Clinton about me. Would they tell about Ross?"

"Never."

"Are you sure?" Hannah nodded and Pokey decided she didn't want to admit she'd blabbed so thoughtlessly. She changed the subject. "Do you . . . play that harmonica much?"

"When I have something to surround. Did it . . . bother you?"

"Well, I'm not used to music. Did you play . . .?"

"Before?"

"Mmmm."

"Oh my, yes. When Lucy and the others . . . after the

end, for a long time all I did was sit in that chair and play. Ate crackers and old apples. Watched the mountain and played. When McQuarter found me, he said he just followed the music."

Pokey could imagine it: the sound snaking out into the town. The man climbing the hill.

"And you made friends, huh?"

"It happens sometimes."

They walked arm in arm, Pokey's heart lightening, despite herself.

CHAPTER EIGHT

Four Small Fish

 SHE FOUND JOHN MCQUARTER BY THE Shenandoah, fishing near Hannah's tree-root seat. He was baiting a hook and paused with a sticky-looking ball of something between his fingers. "Hello. Trouble?"

"Hi. I . . ." The house had creaked frighteningly, though the others hadn't noticed (Ross sleeping as if he had no care in the world, Hannah dozing in the easy chair). Pokey hesitated, her urgency disappearing. "Yes. Maybe . . . I don't know."

The man gave her a quizzical look, squeezed the sticky ball onto the hook, and flicked it out into the water. "Well, then. Tell me."

"Every sound seemed to be somebody coming for Ross. You see, I . . . met the Watson sisters and mentioned him by mistake and they . . ."

John smiled. "Yes? What did they do?"

"They got sort of excited. Said, 'Maybe we should tell Mr. Clinton.' They don't want trouble."

"Hmm." He reeled in his line. The hook was empty. "Not unless they're in the thick of it."

"What do you mean?"

"Maude and Sissy don't like Skip. They wouldn't volunteer to help him. Probably they just felt, as you said, excited. And interested. I'll talk to them."

Pokey was relieved. "You will? That's wonderful. Can you go right away?"

He frowned, sticking another blob of paste on the hook. "No. Don't you see? I'm fishing."

Pokey stood on one foot, then the other. "Yes, but—"

"Anyway, Skip's off walking the track from here to Brunswick. He'll be gone a while. You can relax." He cast out. "Sit a bit."

"Hmm." Pokey peered at his bait can. "What's that stuff?"

"Flour paste and Cheez Whiz. Hannah taught me."

"Oh." Pokey sat on the tree-root seat (it was very comfortable) and leaned back. The river roared and whispered, moving fast while staying the same. It was almost soothing. John McQuarter caught a fish, smacked its head with the side of his hand, and with a satisfied smile dropped it into a green plastic bucket.

Pokey sat up. *That's the way the world really is*, she thought. *Smacked.* "Why did you leave Washington?"

John reloaded his hook, studied the river, sent out the line. "I . . . got tired. Told myself, 'Your term of office is over.' I'd had enough of work and worry; others were willing. Most of the time we didn't agree on what was important, what to do. I said goodbye, tried to find someplace simple, peaceful, happy—"

"With electricity?"

He smiled ruefully. "That was the idea. But maybe I didn't go far enough. Maybe I should load up Hannah, the Watsons, even you, and go . . . out west somewhere."

"They wouldn't go."

"No."

"Do you know what's happening to the children on the trains?" He was cleaning the fish. He looked up, his eyes level, as she continued. "They take them to a university in Ohio. Store them there, in dormitories, drugged in bed, like . . . dead fish." She shuddered and looked away. "Lying in rows. Did you know?"

"No. Are you sure?"

"Ross was there. He saw."

John McQuarter turned away from the water and came nearer. "No," he repeated. "The Children's Concern, they were always so efficient, and . . . concerned." He rubbed his hands across his pants, drying them. "Maybe it's only temporary."

"They're flabby." Pokey stood up.

He winced, shaking his head. "No, that's terrible. How . . . how is Hannah taking it?"

What about me? "She's quiet."

They stood together, watching the river; it didn't begin to soothe her now.

Finally he touched her shoulder. "Come. I'll walk you partway home." He packed up his gear. Pokey picked up a stone, flung it as far as she could.

On the path, the congressman handed her the green bucket. There were four fish in it. "Here. Take these to Hannah for your supper."

"Thanks. Will you come, too?"

"No, I'm going to see"—he gave a little wave—"if I can keep the lid on."

What lid, she wondered, but he was gone.

Hannah was at the kitchen table when Pokey arrived, kneading bread. "Hello," she said, pushing the ball of dough with the heel of her hand, turning and folding it. "Where were you? I was worried."

"I'm sorry. You were sleeping. I went to the river. Here, John McQuarter sent some fish."

Ross appeared at the bedroom door, rumpled and rosy-looking. "Hannah, I can't sleep another minute. Really."

"Four nice ones." Hannah peered into the bucket. "And they're cleaned. Don't know what gets into him. Pokey, put these fish in the refrigerator. We'll have them tonight." She slapped the bread dough a few times, then dropped it in an oiled bowl and draped a dishtowel over. "There." Her hands hovered on the edge of the cloth a minute, then she said, "I'll rinse the bucket," and went outside.

Ross followed, calling, "Can I get dressed?"

"No! Not till tomorrow."

He returned and grinned expectantly. "Well, here we are."

"Um, yes." Pokey sat at the table, scraping a bit of flour with her finger.

"Want to play cards? She has a deck."

"Well, I . . ." Pokey traced the wood grain on the table top. She knew she should talk, be friendly. But she felt too dragged and distant. "Not right now."

"Hmm." He got the cards anyway and sat across from her, holding them. "What's it like at the river?"

"Nice. Fast and noisy. There are rocks . . ."

"Is that where the power plant is?"

"No." She explained about the two rivers: the safe tree-root place on the Shenandoah; the train station, railroad tracks, and power plant on the Potomac. "The town is between them. But you can't go there. It's dangerous." She let her voice trail off, unable to manage a long description. "I'll tell you all about the recordings and everything . . . later. Right now I . . . I guess I'm tired."

Ross looked disappointed. "OK. Sure."

Pokey went into the living room. It was dim and cozy. She glimpsed Hannah on the porch, rocking, and tiptoed to the door.

"Hannah? Are you all right?"

"Yes. Just thinking."

"I know. Me too."

There was a big, flower-covered easy chair in the corner. Pokey sank into it, feeling too worn out to ever move again. Her arms and legs were heavy; her thoughts ground to nothing. She didn't need to tell herself not to think of Washington or Matron Shrank or Ohio State. She didn't need to tell herself anything; even the litany was gone. She stared at the brown-gold fringe on an old lamp, hearing Hannah's rocker, *thump . . . thump*, and the slap of cards as Ross played solitaire. They might have been ten thousand miles away.

She put her head on the arm of the chair, her hand under her cheek, and closed her eyes, seeing slowed-down images of silver light, silver trains, silver fish in green buckets . . . and fell asleep.

When she woke, Ross was kneeling beside her, touching her arm. "Wha—"

"Shh," he whispered. "Listen."

Someone was on the porch, speaking to Hannah. ". . . explained he's sick and that you're nursing him," a man was saying. "They understand."

Pokey said, "That's John McQuarter," and sat up.

"Well, good." Hannah sounded harsh. "Do they understand the rest of it?"

"About the children? I didn't tell them."

105

"The children are being hauled away. I'd hoped it was for a good reason, but it's not. John . . . *why?*"

"Some people were always . . . going off half-cocked. It seems they've taken over."

"They think *food* is unsafe."

"Yes. They probably do believe it. But they're not fools. By proclaiming what's safe and rationing supplies, they keep control. They think they're solving problems: comatose children consume less, and . . . the leadership's time of power is increased."

Hannah's chair creaked loudly. "Disgusting."

"Hannah—"

"What?"

"Don't you do anything crazy."

"Me? Why would I?"

"Because I know you. You won't like this . . . news from outside."

"I don't like it. I can't stand it. I don't know what to do."

"I know. I'm afraid we . . . can't ignore it. But promise you won't do anything until we talk again."

"Oh, John."

"Promise."

She gave a huge sigh. "Very well. I promise."

Unconsciously clutching hands, Pokey and Ross tip-toed back to the kitchen. "Who is that guy?" Ross asked.

"Used to be a congressman. He keeps chickens. He and Hannah are friends. I"—this surprised her—"like him, too." Pokey sat down at the table. She was still feeling a little groggy. "I fell asleep."

"Yeah. So I noticed."

She drew together the cards he'd been playing with, carefully stacking them. They were smooth and normal in her hands. "What's that smell?"

"The bread baking."

"Boy, I must have slept a long time."

He nodded. "You all right?"

"I think so. "I—" Sleeping had helped her accept Ross's story, but it still thrummed in her thoughts, the last thing she had known. She felt as if she had just come out of a long tunnel or surfaced from deep water.

"Want to play cards?" he asked again.

"No. No, I'm all right. Waking up." She stayed at the table, holding the cards, sliding them back and forth. Ross got a magazine (a three-year-old *Time*) and sat near her, slowly turning the pages.

Before long, Hannah came in. "Bread's almost done. Let's start super."

"OK." Ross cupped his hand and added in Hannah's ear. "Talk. Let's jolly her up."

Pokey frowned. *My hearing's not defective.*

"Give a body a minute's peace," Hannah answered, tying on an apron. "Pokey can bread the fish. Ross, you're the fry-cook." She went to the back porch and returned with jars of corn and tomatoes.

Ross poured some oil into the skillet. "Pokey, did I ever tell you about how I wrecked a car in Iowa?"

Pokey looked up, her fingers thick with bread crumbs. "You don't have to jolly me up."

"I know. But you looked so sad. . . . Well, do you want to know or don't you?"

Pokey thought it over. "Yes."

Ross dropped two pieces of fish into the hot oil. They sizzled and spattered, and he quickly turned down the heat.

"I left Denver about a month ago, and on the third day of my trip I was driving down a two-lane road look-ing for a grocery. My car had cruise control, broken. I could get it on but had to fiddle and push the brakes a lot to release it. I shouldn't have been using it, but . . . you know. The highway was so straight and plain. You ever seen those roads in Iowa?"

Pokey couldn't help being interested. She shook her head.

"They're straighter than rulers. So all of a sudden, *wham*! I had a blowout. The car started weaving. I grabbed the wheel, slammed the brakes. It didn't slow down. I swerved into a field and mowed through about an acre of corn before crashing into a ditch. The engine conked."

"What did you do?" Pokey asked.

"I got out. There was nothing, I mean *nothing*, there. The corn had grown and fallen down; it was all brown and spiky, tangled with weeds. There wasn't a leaf moving, and nobody around. I couldn't leave my car, not with the generator in back. Anyway, it was miles to anywhere. I got in again, said a little prayer and the motor started. Tried reverse. The rear wheels spun dirt, they weren't even touching the ground. I was almost turned over in that ditch."

"So?" said Hannah. She was making cream sauce for corn, from canned milk and Crisco, wrinkling her nose at her ingredients. "What did you do?"

"I jacked it up and pushed it back about ten times till I got on level ground. Then changed the tire. Then thunked through the field and kept getting hung up on big spikes of corn. They're stronger than you think. When I got to the highway—"

He stopped to turn the fish, which was very brown. "I'd broken a bunch of stuff underneath. An axle or something in the front end. Besides that, the muffler was dragging. The car shimmied. I could barely stay on the road, but I made it to the next town, rattling and banging. Made a terrible racket. I thought, 'Better trade this junk heap in.' " He grinned. "That was only . . . an expression."

"Wasn't it your pickup?" Pokey asked.

"Nah. A new station wagon. I heard something jingling behind me and saw a wagon pulled by two huge horses with about ten kids hanging over the sides. The lady who was driving said, 'Heard you go by.' That was Alice Bortman."

"Hunh." Pokey was envious. "That sounds like fun."

"Fun!" Ross protested.

Hannah wanted to know, "Who was Alice Bortman?"

"A farmer. It was as much the kids' place as hers. They'd travel around, find livestock, equipment, and people. Bring 'em home and settle 'em in. I helped get the buildings electrified again. Located generators in dairy farms and at the Department of Public Works. We rounded up all the tank trucks in eastern Iowa, filled them with gas and kerosene, and parked them in a row behind the barn. I stayed, doing stuff like that, for a few weeks. It was neat. Mrs. Bortman, she helped me pick out my pickup. At the dealership in Ottumwa. Of course there was nobody there, but the keys were in a cupboard. She got one, too, a blue one. Then it was . . . time for me to move on."

"Why didn't you stay?" Pokey asked. The farm in Iowa sounded very civilized to her.

"Well, I had this idea of going to Washington."

"What a journey," said Hannah. "Mowing a cornfield, jingling horsebells. Mercy. I"—she carried a bowl of stewed tomatoes to the table and felt the top of the bread—"have seldom traveled. Up here as a girl to school, it seemed the start of many journeys but I never left. This bread's too hot to cut, but we'll do it anyway. Supper's ready."

While they were eating, Ross said, "What about you, Pokey? Tell us about your travels."

"Aw. Not me." She took a few bites of the fish. It had little tiny bones and she didn't like it. The creamed corn was better. "I . . . maybe later."

"Many nights . . ." Hannah began as she cut the bread. It was too crumbly for slices, she had to make chunks. "Oh, it was no trip like yours, Ross. But hearing you talk makes me think of it."

She smoothed a napkin between her fingers and wiped her mouth.

"I used to spend full days rocking in a chair with my harmonica"—she flashed a smile at Pokey—"then, restless, I walked out at night. It was the silence that wouldn't let me sleep. No cars on the highway, no trains rattling through. No insects or birds. Only the river to hear.

"I took to prowling all night, staring down the dark railroad tracks, my ear sometimes on the rail trying to catch a sound. I'd haunt the streets, thinking of the past, the future. Many's the night I ended up in the moonlight, banging on the walls of John Brown's fort, calling, 'Old man! What's it come to? What are we to make of this? Old man!' "

Pokey and Ross listened, their forks suspended.

"He didn't come. There are no ghosts to give us answers. In the morning, I'd rock and play, put myself back together."

Pokey smiled. She could imagine Hannah striding through the darkness, shaking her fist at the night. "You're really something."

Hannah snorted. "You didn't eat your fish."

"I had enough."

When dinner was over Pokey took the scraps out to the compost heap and tried to lure the cat. "Here, kitty. Fish," she called, but the animal swished her tail and kept her distance.

When the kitchen was clean and everything put away, Hannah made herb tea and they carried their mugs to the porch. Pokey sat on a wooden stool, her back to the mountain. She put her tea on the floor beside her; she was ready to talk.

"I'll tell you about *my* journey," Pokey said, and the others both nodded expectantly.

"After . . . the cloud came and all that, I . . . stayed by myself. All that next summer and fall. It was OK, I was hardly lonely." She remembered how she had moved around almost in a trance. It seemed very long ago. "When the TV's came on, heat sensitive, and started ordering me around, I didn't pay any attention."

Ross interrupted. "They really worked, just because you were near?"

"It was weapons technology, DOD." She'd gotten this from John McQuarter, but gave Ross a cool look as if she'd known it forever. He seemed properly impressed and she continued. "Along about September, buses began rolling through every day with loudspeakers. 'Come with us,' they'd blare. 'To the city. Food and safety. Shelter and warmth. Winter's coming. Get on the bus. On the bus.'

"I didn't let any of those people see me. I didn't want their shelter or warmth.

"Only . . . when the buses left, I really was alone. Winter did come, and the furnace stopped working. I found this portable heater and warmed the smallest room. Got cans of food from the other apartments. There was this dog that stayed with me and . . . one day he didn't come back. I guess that's when I kind of woke up. There was smoke in the distance, funny smells, often no water. The food was running out. Sometimes I went up on the roof at night and saw lights over toward Washington."

"Spooky," said Ross.

"Yes. Well." She shrugged. "I spent a week or so making up my mind, but"—she thought of John McQuarter—"the TV's had told me what to do. I knew there was help in the city. So early one morning I set off, with all my stuff in a shopping bag."

He wanted to know everything. "What kind of stuff?"

"Clothes. My hairbrush. Pictures and addresses and re—" She laughed shortly, amazed at her past ignorance. She'd brought her old report cards, to prove what grade she belonged in, and never again went to school. "I . . ." She'd lost her place in the story.

"Yeah? OK. So you were walking out with your shopping bag," Ross prodded.

"I went right down the middle of the eastbound lane of Route Sixty-six. It was weird. There were all these empty cars, pushed to one side. And the buildings. I must have passed them a million times before, driving with my parents. But it was like I'd never seen them . . ."

"Our eyes have changed." This from Hannah.

"I guess. Anyway, I came around a corner and . . . there was D.C. The road became a bridge, I could see the Monument and the Kennedy Center. It was all right there. I'd been walking for miles but . . . I wasn't ready. I took an OFF ramp, wandered around on the Virginia side"—she remembered the silent loops of concrete—"and took the next one."

Ross and Hannah were watching her in absolute absorption. Pokey kept her eyes on Hannah's knees. "Even though I knew what had happened, I didn't expect . . . *nobody* to be there. In the middle of the bridge I remembered airplanes. They used to follow the river, because of National Airport. At the Potomac you'd always see one. Low and so big. They were beautiful. Now, I'd . . . hardly ever heard one.

"I went over to the rail and stood looking toward the airport, waiting. I couldn't help it, I was crying." She picked up her tea mug and held it. "Well, after a while, I dried my eyes and sat on the pavement. There was a little crack and way down I could see the river."

"And?" Ross asked. "Did you jump?"

"Of course not. I got up and walked into the city. The bridge took me near the Lincoln Memorial. I went in, looked up at Mr. Lincoln, but he just sat there, stone. I walked along the reflecting pool and collapsed on the steps of the Washington Monument, wondering what to do.

"Then I heard something—people, feet moving—over on Constitution Avenue. I snuck up and discovered a line of kids, two or three abreast. One of them saw me, nudged another. They opened a space and beckoned. So I got in line and . . . went with them."

Ross swung the glider. "Where?"

"The IRS building. They were on their exercise march; they did it every day. The funny thing was, nobody talked. I was so happy to see people, so *ready*, I would have asked a hundred questions. But they knew how to be friends without ever looking right at you or touching you. It was only if you said anything that they pulled away."

Hannah said, "Didn't you ever play?"

Pokey couldn't explain the solemn children, although she had been one of them. "No."

"It's not normal."

"It was easier."

"It only seemed so."

For a few moments no one spoke. Then Hannah changed the subject. "Ross, did those people in Iowa have a cow?"

"Oh, yes, several."

"Hmmm. I'd give a lot for a cow. Imagine: milk, butter, cheese." She leaned forward to touch Pokey's leg. "You could have real cream in your tea."

Pokey couldn't be so easily distracted. "I . . . I can't explain. I went and we . . . we all did the best we could. But now—" She was so grateful to be away from there she had to pinch herself to keep from crying. "I'm so glad . . . can I stay here, always? Please?"

"Yes."

"No, I mean seriously."

"So do I. Of course"—Hannah's face changed—"one thing I've learned . . . you can never be sure. But so long as it's in my power, Pokey," she was whispering, her voice thick with emotion, "yes. Stay."

Pokey bent her head to her mug, spilling a little tea, sure she was covered with safety at last. "Th-thank you."

Ross stared toward the darkening trees, his face unreadable. He didn't seem to hear.

CHAPTER NINE
Rolling

 WATER CHURNING AND WAVES RISING LIKE seasickness. Swirling, deep, with tracings of foam. Pokey woke with a start. This was the closest she'd come to dreaming for a long time and she didn't enjoy it.

She bunched the pillows behind her and sat up, her eyes on the slightly different shade of darkness made by the window. *It's still night*, she told herself, squeezing her arms tightly across her stomach because she was shivering.

Hannah and Ross are downstairs. I can go to them. Or turn on the light and read a book.

Instead, she stared at the darkness, fighting sleep, fighting the worries that threatened her peace of mind. She no longer had any easy words to drive worries away.

What makes you think . . . you can step into another life like you step into somebody else's clothes?

She slipped down a little, pulling at the blanket. *And there's another train coming tomorrow. I'll watch it. . .*

First thing she knew someone was shaking her. "Hey, wake up. Can you find me some clothes? Hannah says I can get dressed."

She burrowed farther into her pillow. "Huh? What time is it?"

"It's morning. Open your eyes."

She did and saw Ross in his bathrobe, barefoot and impatient. "Oh-hhh," she groaned. "I was awake all night. Look in the drawers."

He pulled out a pair of the soft gray trousers and a blue and white workshirt. "Hannah can give me a belt." He patted Pokey's covers. "Go back to sleep."

"Uhhhh . . . OK." She rubbed her eyes as he padded across the room. "I'll take you for a walk later, if Hannah says . . ."

"Sure. Thanks." He disappeared.

"Wait, I'll be up soon," she mumbled, closing her eyes. She wiggled her toes, pushed her hands under the pillow, smiled, and fell asleep again.

Then sat bolt upright. "Oh!" Jumping out of bed, Pokey grabbed her clothes and ran down to Hannah. "Where's Ross?" she demanded, pulling on her socks.

"Went to the river. I told him the safe way. He said you were sleeping."

"Do you think he'd go to the power plant?"

"I wondered. But he didn't ask directions or say a word about it."

"No. I told him yesterday. Did you warn him about the recordings?"

Hannah shook her head. "I told him to go no farther than the Shenandoah. But . . . hurry, girl."

Pokey flew down the trail and through the woods. Ross was nowhere in sight. The tree-root seat was empty. Then from the archway marked RIVER STORY a loud voice cut the air. "The River Story. Two mighty streams—"

116

Pokey dove for cover. The message was long, she suspected. Skip Clinton was sure to investigate.

It stopped.

She peeked out and saw Ross, clinging to a ledge, the loudspeaker broken in his hands. He jumped down and vanished through the archway.

"Ross!" She hurried after him, cautious at the RIVER STORY even though the loudspeaker was in pieces. She spied him down the way and called again, "Hey!"

She was too winded, and frightened, to yell loud. All she could do was run. Reaching the last gate, she saw him cross the green; he walked with a limp. *The idiot.* "Ross!" she hissed.

He didn't hear. Approaching John Brown's fort, he looked at it warily, then set off in the wrong direction, as Pokey had, heading right for the innocent-looking pedestal.

Pokey stopped in the middle of the open green, cupped her hands, and screamed, "Ross! *Stop!*"

He turned, furious, as she ran to him and dragged him into the shadows. "What are you doing?" he exclaimed. "There was a recording back there. What if there's another one? Don't you know this is dangerous?"

"Me?" she squawked, panting. "See that pedestal? *That's* the recording! And Skip Clinton lives in the train station, right up there."

He scratched his head. "Yeah? No kidding." Pokey felt very heroic as he grinned sheepishly. "Thanks."

She accused him. "You tricked us."

"You were sleeping. I wanted to find the power place. I didn't know about the noisemakers."

"They're everywhere. This place is a minefield. What do you want at the power plant?"

"Just to look. I bet I could fix it."

Pokey didn't plan ahead. "I could take you."

"Really?"

"Only you have to promise not to touch anything."

"OK."

"Good. Stay behind me."

"Yes, ma'am."

Pokey wondered if he was being sarcastic. "Quiet," she snapped. *I think I like him better sick.*

No sound or movement came from the station. Pokey inched around the fort, hands out, every sense alert, then tiptoed along the path Hannah had taken across the lawn. Ross stayed behind her, and when she stopped he whispered, "Now where?"

"Sh-h! Straight up the street. But stay on this side. That's what she had me do."

The town seemed deserted until, from beyond the houses, a familiar scratchy voice proclaimed, "These stone steps, constructed—"

"Hide!" Pokey cried.

They leaped behind scrawny bushes and a garbage can by the side of the road. Trembling and holding her breath, she saw Skip Clinton strolling along as if he owned the world. He passed within ten feet of them, gazing up at the sky, which was far and very blue, and began to sing. " 'Oh, bury me not'—"

"Who's that?" whispered Ross.

"Clinton. Shh!"

" 'on the lone Prair-eeee. Where the coyotes howl'—" He kept on singing until he got to the stationhouse and slammed the door.

"That's him? What's he like?"

"I think he drinks." Pokey was weak all over. *Stupid. Stupid show-off. You almost got us caught.*

118

Ross was pale. "We shouldn't have done this."

"No. You better get back." A bell rang at the station. Pokey's heart sank. "Come on. I have something to do."

She pulled Ross out of the bushes, crouched, and led him to the wooden steps. "OK. There aren't any recordings here. Up." She took the stairs two at a time. Ross swayed a little, but he followed.

"Hey, slow down."

Not as healthy as you think you are, huh? Pokey stopped at Main Street. "Hannah's is up that way."

"Where are you going?"

"Don't worry about me. Go on now." She turned and hurried back down to the parking lot.

Where can I hide? she wondered, kneeling in the last row. All she could see was a bit of track and a small space around it. *Where's Skip Clinton?*

The stationhouse door banged; Pokey melted into the side of a car.

The stationmaster was wearing his railroad cap. Holding a STOP sign on a long pole, he walked along the sidewalk and stood with the sign held out at an angle over the track. He stared toward the tunnel, prepared to wait.

Pokey snuck closer, then hesitated. No place was safe. The spaces between cars, windshields, and windows: they were all too open.

Faint and very far away, she heard a whistle.

Then right in her ear someone whispered, "Come on. Let's get in that baggage cart."

It was Ross. "You. Go back."

"Shh!" He jerked his head trainward. "Come on." Heads low, cautiously, they snaked forward to a baggage cart parked near the station.

Skip Clinton stored things there, but he wasn't very

tidy. He had piles of tools and lumber where he could reach them, huge cans of sauerkraut stacked along the side. Farther in, there was a jumble of empty burlap bags and some full ones marked MEN'S SURPLUS SIZE 48.

Ross gently slid a tool box out of the way. He pointed. "Step there," he whispered, and boosted her up. Pokey stumbled; she kept her head down and did as she was told. They wedged through the bags of clothes to the front where there were one-inch slats to peer through.

Skip Clinton stood like a soldier at attention. The track reached across the river to the tunnel; the opening at the far end was light. Empty.

Pokey got nervous. "Oh, Ross, we're so close! This is dangerous."

"You can see, can't you? Now, hush!"

The ground was trembling. The tunnel opening turned black, and a wavery headlight became visible. The rumble increased until, with a shriek of its whistle, the train roared from the tunnel like a stampeding animal.

Brakes squealed. It stopped and stood, shuddering.

Miss Vanderpugh sat in the last car, her eyes downcast. Matron Shrank was standing at the front of the middle one, saying something (probably the litany) and watching with hawklike attention to be sure none of her charges disappeared.

It's all lies! Don't believe her!

The CC leaders, Tom and Helene, were in the first car, leaning out of the door, listening to Skip Clinton.

" . . .worried about that piece of track," the stationmaster was saying, "and I need to show it to the engineer."

"Well, be quick," Helene ordered. "We're on a tight schedule."

120

"Ah, yes. That's what I was wondering. Headquarters told me. You're not bringing the children off the train to take their pictures and say their names?"

"That's right," said Tom.

"But why? I don't understand. It was always so important before. I swept the sidewalk real good, just in case . . ."

Tom shook his head. "We had a big meeting to discuss it. Matron Shrank has accurate lists, they're all we need. After we lost that kid here—"

Helene leaned around him, her glance darting here and there. Pokey froze. Ross grabbed her sleeve; his breathing was strangled. "Shhh." Pokey wasn't sure whether she said it or he did.

"We were being over-efficient," Helene told Skip, smiling down at him. "We'll put identification tags on the kids when we get them settled. That's good enough. Now, why'd you need to talk to Joe?"

"Joe," the stationmaster said blankly. "Oh, the engineer. I want to show him this bit of track."

"What's wrong?" asked Tom. "A problem?"

"It's loose. You know there's no maintenance anymore. With all these trains you should send me a work crew."

Tom frowned. "We don't have any work crews." He waved to the engineer. "Go with Clinton, Joe. See what you think."

Joe, a stout gentleman in a railroad cap and uniform just like Skip's, swung down from the cab and the two of them walked uptrack, talking.

Tom and Helene went inside and sat in the first row of their car.

Ross whispered, "What's that camera?"

"They use it like a telephone. It sent my picture to Washington. My name, too."

"Hmm. See the microphone?" Pokey noticed it for the first time, silver and mesh-covered, mounted right below the camera. Ross's voice got even lower. "Looks powerful. Shh."

"OK."

The train gleamed in the sunshine. In Pokey's memory the children had always been still as statues. But in fact, a number of them were moving around: a girl of four or five with tangled blond curls was rubbing her nose with great concentration; a boy in the second car stood up, received a firm "No!" from Matron Shrank, and sat again, frowning; a boy and girl in the back of Tom and Helene's car pointed at something out the window and giggled.

Pokey didn't see Trudy, but there were others she recognized. Her heart beat faster, and she raked her eyes from car to car. Even the children who were sitting quietly seemed on the edge of animation. *Suppose I just stood up and yelled, "Hey, you guys! Come here. Don't listen to them. It's safer here. Come on!"*

She looked at Ross. He mouthed, "You be quiet," and held her elbow.

"But—" They were so trusting, so unaware. "Oh, Ross."

"There are only six grown-ups," he said, biting each word.

Pokey grabbed his arm. "Don't you do anything!"

Ross shook his head. "I would," he said, but he didn't move.

The train men returned. Promising, "I'll take it easy," the driver heaved himself into the cab.

"Right-o, Joe," answered the stationmaster.

The train coughed steam.

Tom motioned to Skip. "Can you fix that track?"

"I'll try."

He smiled thinly. "Good. How is everything else here? Quiet?"

"Oh, yes. Quiet as a lamb, old Harpers Ferry is. You can depend on that."

Helene signaled; the train started forward.

"Goodbye!" called Clinton, waving and grinning. The machine crept over the odd bit of track, then picked up speed with a cheerful *shriek-shriek* of its whistle.

In the last car, Miss Vanderpugh still had her head bowed. *They shouldn't make her do this. She shouldn't. She should stop them . . . Oh, come back!*

"Hannah!"

Pokey jumped. Hannah had been standing on the other side of the track.

"Hannah Lucas," Skip Clinton repeated, sounding bossy. "What are you doing here?"

She swept across the rails with her head high, her hands in fists. Glared at her neighbor with pity and rage. "You are a fool," she proclaimed.

The man blinked. "Hannah?" She ignored him and he watched her go, scratching his head. Then muttered, "Crazy black woman," and started inside.

"Clinton!" called the man from headquarters, his voice booming out of nowhere. "Step before the camera, please."

The stationmaster obeyed, peering up at the big dark eye. "Yes?"

"I heard the train leave. Who was that you were talking to?"

"A neighbor."

"Neighbor." A familiar clicking started, the electronic files being activated. "What neighbor?"

"Miss Hannah Lucas."

The clicking increased and the man at headquarters said, "Lucas, Lucas. That's one we haven't got a picture of. Get her to stand in the circle."

"She won't," Skip murmured.

"How's that?" the man at headquarters inquired.

"She's gone."

"Clinton, you know we're supposed to have pictures of all your population."

Looking very uncomfortable, the stationmaster said, "I told you before. She won't pose. She went home."

"You getting her moved out of there? Her and the others?"

"Yeah, yeah. Soon."

"We won't wait forever, Clinton. Over and out."

The red lights dimmed, the camera's eye darkened inside. Skip opened his mouth, closed it, and strode out of sight, slamming the stationhouse door.

"Come on, Pokey," Ross whispered.

Pokey nodded but she didn't budge. She was listening to the last sound of the train, as if part of her had been taken with it and the rest couldn't move.

Ross nudged her, pointing to the microphone. "Quiet," he said. Pokey allowed herself to be led. They caught Hannah at the stairs.

"*Sssst!* Hannah!" Ross called. "It's us. Wait."

She stopped. Pokey expected her to scold them, but she smiled. "Yes, we must witness." Taking a few steps upward, she added, "The train goes and we stay here. I should have thrown myself in front of it."

Ross caught her arm. "No, Hannah."

Angry, she pulled away. "I can't stand it. I'm a simple woman." She turned and suddenly, shockingly, spat over the rail. "Pah! They make me sick."

She turned and climbed upward. Pokey hurried after her. "Hannah, you should be more careful."

"Aye," the old woman answered. "So should we all."

At the house they found a note on the door:

> H, P, and young man—
> Come to Jefferson's Rock
> at dark.
> J. McQ.

Pokey grinned when she saw it, then immediately got worried. Things were moving, and slipping away.

CHAPTER TEN

Jefferson's Rock at Twilight

 THE DAY DRAGGED UNBEARABLY. POKEY found a novel, *A Tale of Two Cities*, and tried to read, but she didn't get far. The words kept losing meaning, slipping away, with only tiny glimmers of, *Hey, this is interesting*, that rose and submerged like whales in the ocean.

Finally, twilight came, and Hannah rubbed her hands. "At last. Ready? I'll find the light." She went to the bedroom for the flashlight and got new batteries from the closet shelf. Then clamped a blue felt hat on her head and handed sweaters to Pokey and Ross. "Here. We'll be cold when the sun goes down."

They went partway to the cliff trail, then branched off through an old cemetery to another path that traversed the side of the hill.

"Where does this lead?" Pokey asked.

"To the rock. Then on past the church and down the stone steps."

"Are there recordings?"

"Not up here."

"I could disconnect them," Ross offered.

"You leave them alone."

"Yes, ma'am."

Jefferson's Rock was a boulder out in space, balanced

precariously on a larger rock and man-made columns. Just beside it on the same outcropping was a smooth, flat ledge and standing there, waiting for them, was John McQuarter.

Hannah strode down the last section of the steep trail, with Ross and Pokey scrambling after. The congressman reached out and helped her up as the younger ones hoisted themselves. "Welcome." He shook Hannah's hand, then Pokey's.

Pokey made the introduction. "Mr. McQuarter, this is Ross. He came from Denver."

"Ross Jacobson, sir." Ross shook hands, too; he was blushing.

"Call me John." He winked at Pokey. "You, too."

"Oh. OK." There was a fire ready but unlit in the center of the ledge and a pile of wood off to one side. Pokey stepped over it and walked out to the edge.

The town wasn't visible; only a church steeple gave hint of it. Everything else was wide open, high above the Shenandoah, with another mountain (tall as Hannah's but not so rock-faced) across the way.

"I often come here," John explained. They were all standing silent, awed by the view. "When I need to get . . . perspective. Great hills are a comfort. They are . . . implacable. Let's sit down."

He had brought a pillow for Hannah, and helped lower her onto it, then turned to Pokey and Ross.

"I expect this fire will draw Skip Clinton."

"But, sir—" Ross began.

"And when it does, you slip off the ledge—" He pointed to the hillside. "Into the shelter of the trees."

Ross insisted, "But what if he sneaks up? What if . . ."

"I want to see how he accounts for himself. But don't worry. Skip doesn't come quietly. Does he, Hannah?"

"No. Never."

They sat. Ross kept glancing at the way into town until Pokey assured him, "It's all right. They'd know."

John McQuarter bent to the pyramid of twigs and wood and struck a match. Leaves caught, then the rest. He sat back, cross-legged, and frowned at Hannah, at Ross, then at Pokey.

"I stood in my chicken yard today, thinking I would observe from a secure position the train coming through. And was shocked to see *all* of you running around, endangering yourselves."

Hannah kept her head high, her back straight. Pokey was embarrassed. Ross gulped and began, "I had to protect her, sir."

Pokey winced and sent him a dirty look. "Don't use me for your excuse."

He grinned. "Well, I wouldn't have done it if you hadn't gone first." Pokey was secretly pleased, and said nothing.

Hannah spoke with finality. "We had to watch the train. You know that."

"Yes, I . . . I do," he answered. "And here we are. I think we should begin by telling what we're thinking, each in turn. Hannah?"

She put her hands on her knees and gazed past him to the distant hill. "When all I had were suspicions, I could let the trains go by with only . . . unsettlement in my heart. But now—I cannot stand and watch again. John, I cannot."

"Ross?"

"I'm with her," he said, meaning Hannah. "Whatever you do."

"Pokey?"

"Me? I . . ." Sitting up here, with everyone so serious,

she felt shaky inside. The trees on the far hill faded in the last light. "I keep seeing that train. I'm sorry I ever saw it."

"Humh," John McQuarter grunted, adding wood to the fire. "Don't I know."

Pokey pursued him, feeling edgy. "So? We can't *do* anything, can we?"

Slowly, he began. "As I see it, we have three alternatives." Pokey sat back. This was more like it: solutions. "One is to pick up and leave." He was looking at Hannah. "You and these children, the Watsons, all of us. Pack up and move somewhere else. Forget all this. Leave it to them."

Hannah was shaking her head. "I'll not leave Harpers Ferry. This is my home."

"I thought not. All right, our second choice is to do nothing. Close our eyes and ears. Make some accommodation with Skip. Ignore the trains."

A tremor ran through Pokey's spine. "No," she whispered. Hannah and Ross echoed her, dark as thunderclouds.

"So." John didn't seem surprised. "We are left with one alternative. As Pokey said, to do something. Take some action."

"Hey, wait a minute," Pokey protested. "That's not what I said."

"Forgive me." He shrugged. "I'm out of practice."

Hannah had begun to smile.

Ross said, "I'm ready for anything. But . . . what did you have in mind?"

"I'm not sure." Darkness had come, the flames shone on his face. "I don't know what we could hope to accomplish. Something."

Pokey began to worry. Everyone was so . . . solemn.

Here she was, finally safe and happy, and quick as that, it was slipping away. To make things worse, as if contributing to the fall, she couldn't help speaking. "In Washington, it was easy to believe them; we did what we were told, like we were"—she'd never forget—"puppets." The ledge was cool under her; the fire crackled yellow-white. "We were so scared, and didn't . . . care. It was only the Children's Concerners who . . . seemed awake."

John McQuarter studied his clasped hands. "She's right, you know. The city that got rid of the dead kept the ghosts. I was there. I lived and worked . . . sleepwalking. I saw the obedient lines of children (even a year ago) and never really thought to ask, 'How are they?' We were off-balance somehow, wounded, shocked. And guilty at surviving. We didn't see clearly."

Hannah made an impatient gesture. "It's never easy, seeing clearly. Your CCers are in the dark. Too clever . . . but not solving anything."

Flames danced and skittered and the wind shifted, briefly covering Pokey with smoke. She hunched away from it and squeezed her knees.

Almost to himself, John continued, "I had to leave when I did. I *had* to. But now—"

Pokey nudged a fallen stick into the fire, then heard something. "Shh! Listen."

A faint recorded voice was saying, "These stone steps, hand-carved from a hillside of solid rock—" It was succeeded by another, "Saint Peter's Church—" Above the messages, Skip Clinton could be heard singing, " 'Oh, Shenandooooooh, I long to seeeee you.' "

Pokey and Ross scooted off the ledge and huddled near the curving trunks of trees.

130

The singing stopped. Twigs broke and stones rattled as the man approached. Once, he seemed to stumble. "Ooof!" He swore. "Damned woods."

Then a pause: heavy breathing nearby, a rustle of clothing. Pokey grabbed Ross.

"Hello?" the stationmaster called. "Who's there?"

He stayed out of the circle of firelight until John answered, "It's me, Skip. Come join us."

Skip Clinton lurched into view, carrying a shotgun and a bright-red fire extinguisher. He was out of breath, wheezing. He peered at the two by the campfire. "John? Hannah, is that you?" His laugh was self-conscious. "Heh-heh, it *is* you. I thought . . . trespassers. You really had me going."

"Join us, Skip," John said. "Sit down."

He dropped his equipment, climbed onto the ledge, and stood, swaying. "No. I won't. I . . ."

"Just a cozy fire," John McQuarter assured him. "I wondered, Skip, how you were feeling tonight."

"Pretty good!" He laughed and wiped his lips. (Pokey realized, *He's been drinking.*) Then remembering himself, the stationmaster pulled in his stomach, put his hands on his hips, and accused, "What are you doing, anyway? You're not supposed to be here. Fires are against regulations . . ."

They both looked at him, unwavering.

"*You* are against regulations. You're not supposed to be making campfires, walking around acting like you own the place. You're supposed to be leaving, gone. You tell her?"

John McQuarter shook his head. "No."

"You didn't?"

"*You* tell her."

He stared at Hannah. "Hannah—"

"Evening, Mr. Clinton."

"This morning, you—" He shook his head. "Forget it." He was no longer out of breath. Shifty-eyed, he touched an inner pocket as if for courage. "Hannah, you and Maude and Sissy, and even John, are going to have to move. That's my orders."

"Oh?" She was cold and steady.

"They mean business this time."

"How will you manage it? I've lived here near fifty years. I'm not finishing somewhere else. And Maude and Sissy, you know what happened the last time you tried to get them gone. Remember?"

He didn't answer.

"Didn't they throw water on you and chase you with brooms?"

"There's no need to bring that up." He pouted, shaking his head in the firelight. "I have to do what I'm told, Hannah. It doesn't look good."

"No, it doesn't."

John McQuarter poked the fire. Skip Clinton fumbled with his inner pocket again. "It *is* nice here. Care for a drink?"

"No, thank you," said John. "Sit down."

"Don't mind if I do." Removing a silver flask as he knelt, he offered it to Hannah, "Miss Hannah?"

"No."

He held the flask, balancing it, then took a quick swallow, his head turned slightly away. "We can sit here for now, peaceful." He swallowed again, then burped discreetly. "You don't know how lonely it is, being in charge. You never visit me."

John chuckled. "Sure, we do."

"They need me, them from the city. I'm important. I keep their trains running through."

With that, everyone's attention shifted, intensified. Though Skip Clinton, fiddling with his flask, didn't notice.

John McQuarter said, "Yes. About those trains."

"Did you see the one we had today? A big one."

"I saw it."

"They're clearing out the city, you know. Children," he said with a sneer, as one might say *pus pots*. "Nothing but disease spreaders. Nose-pickers. Things'll be better when they're gone."

"You're wrong," said John.

"What do you mean?"

"What if it's not the children that's a problem, but their keepers?"

"What? What's gotten into you?" He got on his knees, then squatted back on his feet. "You don't know anything. They *told* me."

"What if it isn't true?"

"It *is* true. They're taking them to Ohio. Over on the other side of the mountains. They can stay there. Keep their germs there." He lumbered to his feet. "You get funny ideas, man. You're alone too much. Well, you can keep away from me. Both of you. I don't need your help. Hannah?" He loomed over her, and she glared back, her lips tight. "I haven't forgotten. You were rude to me this morning."

"Never."

"You don't belong at the station. You stay away. I've got another train coming. Tomorrow. Right after dawn. You stay away." With that, he slid down from the ledge, gathered his equipment, and left.

Stones skittered in his path. They heard him pause to drink, with a smacking, "Ahhh." Recordings went on and off in his wake but this time he didn't sing.

In silence, Pokey and Ross rejoined the circle. John said, "I thought we should see . . . what he was thinking. If he had questions. If he might"—he sighed—"be flexible."

Pokey sat cross-legged. The ground was hard. "Is he really going to make you move away?"

"No," Hannah answered.

John held a stick in the flames until it caught, then laid it across the top of the fire.

"Another train?" Ross murmured. "What are we going to do?"

All four sat motionless, close as if they were touching.

Then John leaned away from the fire. "Well, it's settled. I'm going back to Washington."

Pokey was appalled. "What do you mean?"

"It's the only way to stop this. I'll go around, find people, talk to them, explain. I'm sure if people *know*, they'll change."

"The CCers and headquarters won't let you," Pokey insisted, adamant. "They'll lock you up."

"I'll come." Ross nodded earnestly at John McQuarter. "I'll help. If we could get into headquarters we could broadcast over their own system. We could make our own headquarters somewhere. Do things gradually."

"You're crazy," said Pokey. "You can't go back there. You just got here."

"*You* just got here," John said gently. "You can stay."

"But—" Remembering how hopeless the empty streets had always seemed, Pokey had a sudden image of someone running happily, in sunlight, and pushed the thought away.

Hannah interrupted. "City, headquarters—pah! What about tomorrow?"

Pokey was afraid if she wasn't careful, she'd start to cry.

"Now, Hannah," John began.

She overrode him. "We'll stop the train."

Ross grinned. John protested, "But—"

Pokey's heart leaped. "Could we?"

"Yes, indeed. And tie up ol' Skip Clinton with ropes." Hannah laughed. "No more trains will come through here. That's one small thing," her voice dropped, "that *I* can do."

John leaned forward, reaching out to her. "I knew you'd suggest this, Hannah. But there are problems."

She put hands on her hips, not interested in problems. Pokey asked, "What?"

"The camera and microphone pick up everything. If headquarters gets wind of trouble, they'll send help. They're always on the lookout."

"Well," Pokey was thinking fast, "we'll shut off Skip's breaker. The one with the pink ribbon."

John shook his head. "Sorry. If the hydroelectric plant goes down, or seems to, they'll be out here even faster. We need *time*. Not an army swooping down on us."

Ross was smiling. "How about . . . just the microphone?"

John McQuarter looked up. "How's that?"

"If we stay out of the circle, out of the camera's range, and the microphone isn't working, no one will know what we're doing. Everything will *look* all right."

John squinted, considering. Hannah beamed at Ross and said, "I knew first time I saw you, you were special."

Pokey told the congressman, "He's good. Disconnected that RIVER STORY thing right while it was talking. Wired up a whole town in Iowa . . ."

"A town?"

Ross ducked his head, shy for a minute. "Uh, yes." Then he straightened and took a deep breath. "Yes. I know I could do it. Piece of cake. The incoming voice from head-quarters, too. You'd probably want them on two switches."

"Huh." John McQuarter sat back and repeated, "Hunnh. What do you know?"

"Yes," said Hannah. "You see? This is becoming . . . sensible."

"And what would we do with the kids?" Pokey asked. "Bring them here to live?" She multiplied in her head: sixty or eighty to a car, times three cars, makes . . . "A hundred eighty or two hundred forty. Would they stay here?"

Hannah blinked. "Why, I'm not sure."

Pokey thought of the town water supply and Hannah's stores of food. They wouldn't last long.

"Uh . . . two hundred?" John asked. "That many? Well . . . We'll think of something. Eventually, we'll have to go to Ohio, wake those children, treat 'em right. Get all of them going, doing things, growing things. Working."

Peeling potatoes, Pokey thought with a quick private smile.

"The kids in Iowa do everything," Ross said. "Other places, too, I bet. We could figure out ways to travel and go see."

"We're getting ahead of ourselves," John warned. "If we get to the place where we have to worry about the kids, we'll be . . . home free. Hannah?"

"Yes." She was stuck where she had been a few minutes before. "Tomorrow. We stop the train." She was sitting tall, her arms folded in front of her like an ancient priestess. "Agreed?"

Pokey stared at the fire. Trains, rows of children, TV's spouting instructions, CCers in sturdy jumpsuits: they were moving, blind, never interrupted. "If we could do it—wouldn't they be surprised?"

The others were waiting. Pokey wasn't as certain as Hannah or Ross, but she couldn't help smiling as she ignored her doubts and said, "OK. I'm with you."

"OK!" said Ross. "Now, can you take me somewhere, sir? I'll need to find a good hardware store. For switches."

"Uh . . ." John wasn't used to hurrying. "There's my old station wagon, but . . . it's out of gas."

Ross was practically bursting. "I could fix that."

John scratched his head. "I bet you could. All right. We'll go—may take some looking. Hannah?"

She was distracted, thinking. "Yes. You go on. We have a lot to accomplish, a lot to plan. Pokey and I will begin. We'll work out how to capture prisoners from the train."

Pokey felt weak. "We will?"

John stood up, brushing his pants. "Hannah, will you tend the fire? I brought some sand."

"Of course."

He slipped over the side and heaved a heavy bucket onto the ledge. Ross hit Pokey's shoulder. "See you later."

As they went away, Pokey heard Ross ask, "Tell me, sir. Where were you a representative from?"

They were almost out of hearing distance.

"Michigan. And call me John, will you?"

Hannah hadn't moved. Pokey lugged the bucket closer and sat down. "I never thought it would mean going back."

"You don't have to. You can choose."

"To stay or go? But I—I don't know."

"You'll know . . . likely . . . when it's time."

Pokey wasn't so sure. She hugged her middle and looked from the dying fire up to the sky, where stars were coming out. *If I could take it all back, squash the plans . . . Would I? Have everything stay like it is?*

No. "Oh, Hannah. Matron and the other CCers, they're strong."

"Yes. And, I believe"—the woman stood and knocked the fire into embers, sprinkling them with sand—"so are we."

CHAPTER ELEVEN
Night

THE FLASHLIGHT BEAM DANCED IN THE trees, throwing shafts of white. Pokey held Hannah's arm. When they got to the house, she was surprised, for Hannah said, "Leave the sand bucket and pillow here. We'll go right on."

"On? Where?"

"We have to enlist help."

"An army," said Pokey, "at least."

"That would be hard to find. What we do have"—she pulled her hat more firmly onto her head—"is the sisters."

"Do you think so?"

"Yes, indeed. Come, it's getting late." With long strides she set off, and soon the Watsons' house loomed before them. Every light was on, upstairs and down; it looked like an ocean liner ready to sail off the edge of the cliff.

"That's funny." Hannah hurried to the door and knocked loudly. "Hello!"

The door opened an inch, then flew wide to show the Watson sisters, both very agitated and clutching brooms.

"Oh, Hannah," Maude wailed. "Thank goodness you're here."

"We came to your house but couldn't find you," Sissy added, her face flushed.

Hannah stepped into the hallway. "Well, I'm here now," she said. "What's wrong?"

"Something terrible," Maude told her, shaking her head and holding her broom tighter. "Skip Clinton came. More obnoxious and unreasonable than ever. He . . . seemed angry. Said he'd seen you. Said we have to move to Washington. This time he means it. All of us. He'll use—"

"Force if he has to," Sissy finished. She looked around her hall, which had pictures of flowers on the walls and a soft, woven rug on the floor. "We . . . get along here. Why do we have to go?"

"Hunh," said Hannah, more a grunt than a word. Pokey winced, afraid this trouble was her fault, for being here, getting headquarters interested when she was "lost." She tried to stand tall, as if she could shoulder plenty of responsibility, but she was worried.

Hannah went on. "Maybe we can solve two problems at once. Put Skip in his place"—her eyes flashed—"and more."

Sissy's chin came up, Maude's, too, in exactly the same gesture of interest and defiance. "Oh?" said Maude.

"Yes," Hannah replied. "I'm afraid there's trouble in Harpers Ferry, and we need your help."

Maude put aside her broom, and Sissy said, "We're not going to move away."

"You don't have to," Hannah said. "Let's talk." She led the way into the living room as if the house were her own. Maude and Sissy settled side by side on the sofa. Hannah took a straight chair. Pokey hovered beside her, too nervous to sit.

"Here's the story," Hannah began, then described the train, its destination, the situation in Ohio and in the city. The Watsons nodded, yes, no, yes, intent on every word. Pokey was astonished at how quickly they understood.

Maude said, "That's awful. Bunch of nuts."

Sissy's head bobbed with sympathy. "Glad *you* got away, girl."

Pokey stammered, "Th-thank you."

When it came to solutions they were willing and curious.

"What do you have in mind?" Maude asked.

"Well, I . . ." Hannah looked uncertain for the first time. "I can't promise we'll make it. But I want to stop the train. Get the leaders off it—there's usually five of them, plus Skip—and hold them somewhere, prisoner."

"Six, then?" said Maude. "Good. We have a wonderful garden cart. Easily handles two or three hundred pounds. We can move them in that."

"Perfect." Hannah rubbed her hands, smiling.

"We won't have to . . . kill them, will we?" Sissy was very serious. "I wouldn't . . ."

"No. Never. John is our druggist. I hope he'll find an anesthetic." Hannah leaned forward, careful to explain everything. "Listen . . . John wants to go to Washington, to talk to people there. It's a long shot, might work. Anyway, he says he has to. *I'm* worried about *here*. Skip Clinton"—she must have known the Watsons would like this part—"needs a comeuppance. And the trains must be stopped. Here, at least. It's little enough, but that's what I want."

Maude went to Hannah and stuck out her hand. "Count me in."

"Me too," said Sissy from the sofa, twisting her skirt and blinking her eyes as if dealing with tears.

"What do we do?" Maude asked. "And when?"

"Come to my house two hours before dawn. With your garden cart."

At the door, Sissy gave Pokey a quick kiss. "Poor dear. Don't you worry." She managed a wobbly grin. "We'll fix 'em."

"Remember to be quiet," Pokey warned.

Maude stepped onto the porch, shaking a finger at Pokey. "Young lady, we're not incompetent."

"Now, Maudie," Sissy crooned, pulling her sister inside. "Relax. She's new here. Doesn't know us." She slammed the door.

Pokey and Hannah watched the house for a minute. Lights went off, one by one, until only a few remained. "Will they be OK? They seem excitable."

Hannah started walking. "They'll be fine." Halfway down the block she muttered, "I think."

At home, Hannah sat at the table with a battered Spiral notebook and a pencil stub. She wrote at the top of a clean page: GET, and in the second column: REMEMBER.

Pokey hung around the kitchen for a while. Hannah wrote TAPE in the GET column and nodded to herself, making small doodles in the corner of the page.

Pokey began feeling nervous. *Tape? What do we think we're doing? Who do we think we're kidding?*

She left the kitchen and went out to the porch. It was dark but she sat in the rocker and looked out in the direction of Hannah's mountain. *This is happening too fast. I'm not ready.*

She rocked and rocked until her eyes grew accustomed to the night and she could see the outline of the steep cliff against the sky.

Why not? Surprised at herself, she found the idea of

taking action against the CC, or at least the train, was exciting as well as frightening. And the thought of going back . . . *Better be careful.*

When Hannah appeared, she had a towel wrapped turban-style around her head. "Still out here? You all right?"

"Yes. I was scared for a while, but . . . not now."

Hannah smiled. "It comes and goes."

"What's that on your head?"

"I washed my hair. So I won't have to think about it, in the raid."

"Is that what this is?" Pokey asked. "A raid?"

"That's what I've been thinking," said Hannah. "A new raid at Harpers Ferry. Of course, I'm just a foolish old woman, but the notion pleases me."

Pokey felt cold. "What happened to the other raiders —John Brown's?"

Hannah hesitated. "They died. But they changed things. Nothing was ever the same again."

Pokey found she had lost her voice. Hannah stood at the top of the steps, looking out at the darkness. After a while she said softly, "See out there? It's a raider's sky."

"What's that?"

"Deep and so clear. But it's really"—she banged her chest with a fist—"in here. When you know it's time. You have to act."

Hannah held a porch column and something in her stance made Pokey whisper, "Are you scared?"

"Hmm." The woman turned and touched Pokey's sleeve. "Like I said, it comes and goes. Now, where could Ross and John be?"

"It's taking them a long time. I'm worried."

"So am I. Let's go inside."

They sat at the kitchen table, each lost in her own

143

thoughts, until they heard the car. Then both jumped and exclaimed, "Here they are!"

The men came in the back door, Ross carrying a box. He gave Pokey a thumbs-up signal and a big smile. John said, "We've been all over the countryside. Went all the way to Winchester—"

"But we found 'em," Ross boomed. "Just what we need. I hope."

"Good." Hannah was tapping her notebook. "Are you ready then, John? We have to go."

"Go?" he asked. "Go where?"

"Charles Town." She explained to Pokey and Ross, "That's the nearest big town. John and I've been back a few times. It's still there. Used to have a racetrack, and feed stores. I need burlap bags, belts—"

"Tape," said Pokey.

"Yes. And, John, do you know of a way to render people unconscious besides, ah . . ."

Uneasily, Pokey finished for her. "Bare hands."

He nodded. "I've been thinking about that. We can talk as we drive."

Ross announced, "I'm coming with you."

"No," Hannah said firmly. "It's late. You've been sick. You have to sleep. I need you and Pokey alert and strong in the morning." She gave Ross his medicine and pointed to the bed.

He refused. "In a minute."

Pokey said, "Hannah? I—I can't sleep upstairs."

"Go in the bedroom. Take my easy chair. I've been sleeping in it lately. It's comfortable."

Hannah and John left. Ross sat at the kitchen table; Pokey could tell he didn't want to talk.

Pokey took off her shoes and got into Hannah's bedroom chair with a quilt. She listened to Ross in the kitchen, sorting through the contents of his box, getting something from the refrigerator. Finally, he turned off the lights and climbed into his bed. Then whispered, "Pokey?"

"Yes?"

"Are you awake?"

"Yes."

"I . . . whaddaya think about this?"

"I'm not thinking. If I think I'll get scared."

"Oh." There was a long pause, then he said, "I'm worried. I mean, I'm not sure if I can work the wires; I wish I could turn off the power for a few minutes. I can manage without that, but it's tricky."

"You can do it. You said so. You did before."

"I know, but . . ."

"Did you get the equipment you need?"

"Yes. Switches made for that kind of work."

"See? You're just getting anxious. Think about something else."

After a long while he said, "Like what?"

"I don't know . . ." She tried to think of peaceful, easy things, old, old memories. "Think about the ocean. Did you ever go there? How the waves keep coming, how it sounds . . ." She rearranged herself. "Or birds. Think about how birds used to chirp in the morning. Remember?" He didn't answer. "When I was little one summer there was this bird, right outside my window. Every morning when it was still dark, it would start to sing, 'Cheep-cheep,' and carry on. Woke me up every time. I'd think, 'Go back to sleep, dopey, it's not time yet,' but the bird didn't stop. Pretty soon it had all the others awake and they'd sing, too. Thousands of birds in all the trees. Then—eventually—it really would be morning. I—I can't remember if they chirped all day or if they stopped in the afternoon." His breathing had deepened; he was sleeping, but she continued anyway. "Or think about when you were driving . . . what the countryside looked like. You told me about Iowa . . ."

She closed her eyes. *Oh, please, please. Let us be all right* . . .

It seemed only minutes had passed when Hannah wakened them. The Watson sisters had arrived, wearing identical blue sweatsuits. Hannah was in her Nike hightops; John looked as if he had slept in his clothes.

Pokey dressed hurriedly as John said, "Morning. Let's go over the plans."

CHAPTER TWELVE
New Raid

 THEY WERE IN THE TOWN BEFORE DAWN.

Ross and Hannah went silently to the recordings, disconnecting each one. Maude and Sissy crouched behind a blue van with two flat tires that had stood in the front row of the parking lot for years.

Pokey and John approached the rear of the station-house. "Turned cold in the night," John murmured. "You warm enough?"

Pokey nodded. She was far from noticing anything so simple as the weather.

"Here. Stop a minute." John opened a red backpack. Pokey hugged her elbows and watched. "Here's the anesthetic. You're sure you can handle it?"

"Yes." *If we could get started.*

The pack was filled with small plastic bags, round like popcorn balls, each stuffed with permeated cotton and sealed tight. The bags were squishy with trapped air. Pokey wanted to experiment with the green plastic twist-closers to make sure she could open one fast, but John dropped the backpack on the hood of a car and gestured with his head: *Come on.*

Pokey put the plastic bags in her pocket and followed

147

him around the station to the far side, nearest the tunnel. She studied the front of the stationhouse. Halfway along was Skip's door. Beyond that, the TV camera and microphone were mounted under the wide overhanging roof. The camera pointed downward, away from the door, focused directly on the white circle painted in the middle of the sidewalk. The microphone hung beside it, electric ears keen in every direction.

Pokey was going to ask, "Can it hear us *breathe*?" but John went *sh-h* with his finger.

She knelt and leaned against the building for balance. *How do we know headquarters will wake him? What if they don't? . . . Well, John says they will . . . What if they did already? What if we're too late?*

John was chewing a knuckle, his eyes fixed on the pavement in front of him. Pokey stilled her fears and listened.

Inside, Skip Clinton was snoring. "*WHOOT-wheeeeeeee, WHOOT-wheeeeeeee.*"

"Clinton!" a voice called. Pokey almost screamed, then tensed. Her knees cracked. "Clinton, wake up now. Skip Clinton, do you hear me? . . . Clinton!"

The bedsprings groaned, and Skip Clinton, too. "Ugghhhh."

Pokey peeked cautiously between a garbage can and the wall. The door opened and Skip emerged in his nightclothes (baby-blue boxer shorts and a dingy T-shirt) and bare feet. "Yeah, yeah. I'm coming." He stepped into the circle and looked up. "Here I am."

"Good. Good morning, Clinton." The man at headquarters sounded wide awake. "Too dark to really see you. The train just left. It'll get to Harpers Ferry in about an hour."

"Ah, OK," said Skip, rubbing his eyes.

"The track fixed?"

"Well, it's cold this morning. I better check it. You want me to call back?"

"Naw. There's nothing I can do. If you've got a problem, stop the train."

"Right-o."

"The bell will ring when they pass Brunswick."

Skip Clinton let out a huge, shuddering yawn. "O . . . howaaaaa . . . K."

"Wake up, Clinton."

"Yeah, yeah." He gave a little wave and wandered back into the stationhouse.

John held Pokey's sleeve and they slid softly along the front of the building to the door. *Wait*, he said with his hand.

They could hear the stationmaster moving inside. Pokey touched the ball of anesthetic and loosened the seal. A pungent trail rose and she quickly closed the bag.

John whispered, "Now," and they stepped through the door, closing it firmly behind them to muffle sound. Skip Clinton's living quarters were in the old waiting room. He was in the bathroom; Pokey could hear him brushing his teeth. She and John crept to either side of the door and waited. Pokey was so tense it seemed that everything in the world was focused on the sounds in the bathroom and the one scrap of threshold before her eyes. Then Skip Clinton stepped out.

John grabbed him from the side. "Huh?" the man exclaimed, struggling to see. "John?" Pokey fumbled with the plastic bag, got it open, and holding her breath, shoved it into the stationmaster's face with two hands.

"Huhhh," he said again, staring at Pokey in shock. He

149

took a deep breath as if to speak and, reaching for her, crumpled.

That fast, it was done. The man was breathing (Pokey checked to be sure) but limp and unconscious. She squeezed the plastic bag tight. Belatedly, she was shaking.

"Well done," said John, easing him down.

"So fast?" Maude asked, tiptoeing into the room with Sissy and Hannah. "He didn't know what hit him."

They all eyed Skip with concern. Lying in his own living room in his underwear, he seemed vulnerable and a lot smaller. Then he groaned and Pokey's heart bumped.

"Another whiff, girl," said Hannah.

Pokey bent and pushed the bag to the fallen man's nose. His face grew even more slack. Closing the bag, she looked away, feeling sorry for him. *Maybe I'm not made for this kind of work.*

Ross came in, carrying his box of equipment, a can of spray paint on top. He glanced at Skip and shifted his gear so he could give Pokey his thumbs-up signal. "One down," he said. "Way to go."

"Yeah," said Pokey.

Ross turned to the rest of the group. "I painted a wider circle"—he waved the spray-paint can—"showing the outer limit of what I figure the camera can see. Don't go inside it."

Pokey went to the door. The circle was brown, blending in with the color of the pavement and stretching from the edge of the sidewalk where the track began all the way around to the stationhouse wall. "We can't *ever* go to the parking lot that way."

"No. You'll be seen. Got that, everybody?" All the women and John McQuarter nodded seriously. "Good. I'll work on the switches now." Pokey crossed her fingers and raised them for him. Ross grinned and disappeared up the small staircase near the office.

The five raiders looked at each other. John said, "Now. I've found my old watch. Still works. Skip's office clock said five-forty-eight when headquarters called. Now it's six-oh-six." He set the watch and shook it. Pokey's hands got sweaty. There was so much to do. She didn't want to think about being scared, not for a minute. John continued, "I'll get the car."

Pokey rushed to say, "I'll come, too."

Hannah nodded. "We'll guard Skip," she said, and took a roll of tape from her pocket. "Come on, girls, let's tie him up."

Pokey took the extra plastic bag out of her pocket. "Here. Take this if you need it."

She and John ran through the parking lot and down into town. The recordings were all disconnected; no need to worry and dodge. They turned right and trotted up Main Street around the bend to a tree-lined spot where John McQuarter had left his big gray station wagon, crammed full in back, with Maude Watson's garden cart tied to the roof.

Pokey was panting. "That's a steep hill."

"Yes . . ." John was breathing hard, too, leaning against the car. "Did . . . did you hear Ross? Did he call?"

"Not yet."

They waited and in a minute, the voice came. "OK! Got it! Sound's off."

John looked at Pokey, frozen.

Pokey crossed her fingers and hollered, "Ross! You sure?"

"Yes! Come on!"

John McQuarter wiped his forehead. "Let's go."

151

Pokey got in the front seat. It had been a long time since she'd ridden in a car; the seat felt comfortable, familiar, her feet just fit. The dashboard was layered with dust and she rubbed across it with her fingers, making a streak. John started the engine with a roar, tooted the horn once, and rolled down to the station.

Maude and Sissy were waiting. "Hannah's watching Skip," Maude said. "Let's get the cart down." John did that while Pokey opened the rear door and helped Sissy pull out burlap bags, more tape, and stiff leather belts.

"Put it in the blue van," said Sissy. "That's our supply wagon." Then she and Maude took one burlap bag and a set of belts and headed for the station with their cart.

"Come on, Pokey," said John. "Let's go." They climbed in the car and drove down the street to the corner where John turned, bumped over a curb, and backed across the grass to John Brown's red brick fort.

Unloading beams, plywood, brackets, hammers, nails, Pokey noticed the sky. Their hour was going fast. It was light now. Sometime when she wasn't looking, morning had come. When almost everything was piled near the fort, John pointed toward the station. "Here they come."

Hurrying toward them were Maude and Sissy, pushing the garden cart at an alarming speed, with Hannah jogging alongside holding Skip Clinton's foot. The stationmaster was covered from head to knees with a burlap bag. He almost filled the cart, his feet protruding high in the forefront in rumpled brown socks.

The threesome lurched over the curb and kept on running; the grass hardly slowed them down.

"Told you we could do it!" Maude exclaimed. She was breathless and flushed. "Skip wasn't too heavy. Why, I've hauled rocks that were worse!"

"For the fishpond," Sissy explained. "Now, where should we put him?" The fort consisted of two small rooms, with a solid brick wall between them. Sissy peered into both and proposed, "The smaller?"

"Fine," said John.

The inert stationmaster was tipped out of the cart. Hannah arranged him so he was lying flat, adjusting the burlap bag near his face to give plenty of air room. "Poor man," she said.

Maude and Sissy shook their heads at him. "You should have listened to somebody else," Sissy scolded the silent bundle. "Like us, for instance."

"What is it you have in those Baggies?" Maude asked Pokey. "Powerful stuff."

"John gave it to me," she answered.

"It's actually veterinary," he told them. "For horses. Works fast and suppresses brain function for hours." John glanced at his watch. "We better keep moving."

Hannah said, "There's something I need, John. Can you drive me to the house?"

"I was going to help Maude and Sissy," he said. "Pokey, can you?"

"Sure."

"Don't worry," Maude proclaimed. "Give me a hammer."

John and Hannah drove off. In no time, with Pokey fetching and holding things, Maude and Sissy had nailed heavy plywood over the windows and fashioned door bars with steel brackets and heavy wooden beams.

"There!" said Maude, brushing off her hands. "That's done."

Pokey went into the fort one last time. Skip hadn't moved.

Walking back to the station, Pokey complimented her companions. "You sure are good carpenters."

"Yes, indeed," said Maude.

"We do everything now," Sissy added. "Even built our bird feeders ourselves."

Pokey remembered the platforms surrounding their house. "Do birds really come? I'd love to see one."

"Three last winter," Sissy bragged. "And Maude says, if we wait, we'll surely see a robin."

Ross was waiting outside the station. "How's the fort? Need any help?"

"Nope," said Pokey. "They fixed it. How are your switches?"

"They're both hooked up. I left the incoming broadcast wire on for now, so we'll hear if headquarters calls. When I go back upstairs—" He pointed. There was a small open window high on the parking-lot side. The wires for the equipment under the roof passed by it, and Pokey could see the new switches, in plain view.

"Is that where you'll be?"

"Yes. When it gets close to time, I'll go up and put the mike on, too. So when the bell rings at Brunswick, the sound will come through like it always does. Then . . . when the engine comes, I'll leave the switch on for as long as I can before the brakes squeal. It'll sound like the train passed on by." He looked worried. "I hope."

Maude was eyeing him with admiration. "Smart young fellow," she said.

"Hmm." Ross blushed and went on. "Once I'm up there, I'll flip the incoming broadcast switch from time to time so we'll know if they're calling Skip. Then, if . . . everything works out and we do leave on the train, one of you should put the mike back on. It's the red switch."

One was red, the other white, easy to distinguish. "Pokey, will you?"

Pokey couldn't look at him. She said, "N-no."

"Why not?"

"Because, well," she whispered, "I haven't decided. Maybe I'll come with you."

He squinted. "Yeah? Good."

She backed off quickly. "Maybe not, too."

Sissy patted her shoulder. "Don't worry, dear. If you don't turn the switch, the red one," she said as she stared, fixing it in her mind, "I will."

Pokey said, "What time is it, anyway? Aren't we running late? Where's Hannah?"

"She'll be here," Maude replied. "Come on, Sissy, make sure we're ready." She pushed the empty garden cart to a spot behind the blue van and counted the supplies of bags and tape. "All set."

"Ready?" said John, and Pokey jumped. Hannah was just behind him.

"Yes, sir," said Ross. "What time is it?"

"Six-forty. I better get changed."

"I better go upstairs."

The men went into the stationhouse and Pokey turned to Hannah. "Are we really?"

The woman smiled. "Ready? Yes."

"I . . . I'm not sure what to do, after—"

"You'll know. There's a bit to come, between."

"A bit? A mountain." The train was coming closer. There was no holding it back, or stopping, now. "The plan worked with Skip."

Hannah nodded. "We've just the hard part left."

John came around the stationhouse in Skip's railroad suit and cap.

Pokey whistled. "Is that you?"

"Looks OK, huh?" he asked.

Hannah said, "Perfect."

Ross leaned out the window. "All right, everybody! I'm turning the microphone on. Quiet now."

They waited. Pokey stayed near Hannah, wishing she could hold on to her, bury her head somewhere, run back to the house and hide in bed. The sisters talked softly; John paced on tiptoe; Hannah gazed through her fingers, up beyond the railroad tracks and river to her mountain.

Then, so sudden that it seemed to smash the air, the bell rang, *ding-ding-ding-ding-ding*.

John McQuarter looked pale. Pokey felt a wave of nausea, like blindness washing over her. She stumbled and caught Hannah's arm. "Whoo-oo now," Hannah murmured, and hugged her tight. "We'll be all right."

John came over to them. "You all set?" Hannah nodded.

Pokey patted her chest and stomach. *What do I need? The anesthetic!* She ran behind the station and got the red backpack. *Hurry, hurry.*

Maude and Sissy winked simultaneously. Hannah and John embraced, then she straightened his cap, patted his shoulder, and stepped between cars, out of sight. Pokey glanced at Ross. He gave a thumbs-up sign and Pokey matched it, barely breathing.

They were ready. Pokey crouched with the Watsons behind the van. *Why is it taking so long? What if . . . I can't? What if I'm . . . too little? . . . I can, I can . . .* She memorized the creases in Sissy's sweatsuit. *Oh boy, I hope I don't forget anything.*

The train shrieked, the ground rumbled. Pokey realized that Maude was holding her hand.

John McQuarter stood by the track in Skip's clothes and cap, the big red STOP sign held high. The train came slowly, then slammed on its brakes and the wheels screamed. Pokey saw Ross flip the switch. He winced with fright but shrugged: *Maybe.*

"What's this?" asked the engineer.

"Come here, Joe," John ordered in a low-pitched, false-sounding voice. He motioned and walked away from the train.

Tom and Helene appeared at the first car's door. "Hurry it up," Helene called.

Frowning, Joe jumped down.

"We've got some trouble here." John led him into the parking lot to a spot by the van.

"Ooof!" Joe coughed as John McQuarter attacked with a sharp blow to the stomach. Pokey was quick. She glimpsed the man's big hands and pushed a fresh bag up to his nose.

"Oh-hhaaaaag," he said, collapsing. Behind them, Sissy giggled.

"Get to work, girls," McQuarter ordered. "Pull him out of the way. OK, Pokey, I'll see who's next."

He'd changed from sickly white to rosy red, and Pokey realized he'd been quite nearly scared to death. She couldn't help grinning as he sauntered toward the engine, head down, as if searching for something. From the first car, Tom inquired, "What's up? What's the trouble?"

The mock railroad man scratched his head. "You'd better . . ." then waited.

Tom and Helene gazed down, unsuspicious.

"Um . . . can you come here?" John continued tentatively. "We've got a bit of a problem. You'd better see."

They followed. At the van, John turned, grabbing both their arms and jerking high. They were faster than the engineer. "What?" Tom shouted. "Watch out!" In good physical condition, they flailed their fists and kicked. Pokey ducked and wove, helpless. Then she found an opening and reached Tom's face. He breathed in, his eyes huge with shock, and sagged. Hannah appeared with Helene in an armlock.

"You, you, who are you?" the CCer cried to John. She stopped struggling and stared. "Have I seen you before? Where?"

"Pah." John sounded harsh. "Pokey, take her away."

Helene started fighting again, but Pokey got the bag open and held it high. The smell made her cough. Helene's eyes rolled up and she sighed, "Aaaaaaa," and fell.

The sisters had loaded Joe into the cart. Pokey heard gravel crunch, and voices. "Careful! Oops! Here we go!"

"They should be more quiet," she whispered to Hannah.

"We're almost done. Let's bag these two."

Pokey helped fasten Tom's wrists behind him, then Helene's, and held each one as Hannah hauled more tape around chest and arms, thighs, knees, ankles: no room for wiggling free. She tugged burlap bags over them and added belts, two for each, cinched tight. "There."

"We fixed them." Pokey was exhilarated.

Hannah sat back on her haunches, her face shining with pleasure. "Yes."

John had been checking the engine to be sure no one else was in the cab. "Come on, Pokey," he said. Pokey headed for him, then gasped. Matron Shrank had stepped down from her car and was striding forward. She walked right across the sidewalk, through both circles, under the camera, demanding, "What's going on here?"

Pokey cried, "Go back!"

Instead, Matron snatched and shook her. "What are you doing here? Pokey Hughes. Where did you come from?"

Pokey opened her mouth but she couldn't speak. She couldn't move.

"Here now, what's this?" John grabbed Matron from behind.

She loosened her hold on Pokey to shove at him. "Who are you? What's going on here? Where are . . ."

Pokey glimpsed several children, watching frightened at the train windows. She got hold of a bag, tore it open with her fingernails, shoved it toward the woman's face. For a moment it didn't faze her. She was still shaking Pokey like a rag doll with Pokey's upraised hand flapping in her nose. Then she smiled, continuing, ". . . are . . . my . . . friends?" and fell.

Matron Shrank lay crumpled, her hat off, skirt up, gray coat twisted around her. Hannah rushed over, and she and John and Pokey clutched each other in fear. Pokey quaked. "She walked right under the camera."

At the high window, Ross was white-faced. John nodded and he flipped on the incoming broadcast switch.

The man from headquarters was calling.

"Hello? Matron Shrank, was that you? . . . What's going on there? Matron Shrank? Clinton . . . Clinton? Something's wrong at Harpers Ferry . . . Clinton? Skip Clinton, come in. Clinton . . . hello?"

CHAPTER THIRTEEN
Eastbound Train

 Ross cut off the sound.

"What are we going to do?" Pokey wailed. Several of the children on the train were standing up, clustered at the windows. Any minute they were likely to pile off, mill under the camera, and really ruin everything.

"You stay here," John ordered, fumbling to get a bag out of Pokey's pocket. "Keep her back." He dashed around the rear of the station and Pokey saw why he was running: Miss Vanderpugh had gotten off the train and was hurrying forward.

"Miss Vanderpugh!"

"Pokey?" She broke into a trot, nearing the circle.

"*Stop!* Please, stop!"

Miss Vanderpugh stumbled. "What?"

"See that circle? Don't come in it! Please!"

The woman stood swaying, looking from the circle to Pokey and reaching out her hand as if to test the clear air between them.

"Th-the camera. It'll see you. Please don't . . ." She saw John McQuarter sneaking around the corner and was unable to say more.

He grabbed. "Good job, Pokey."

Miss Vanderpugh screamed, "What? What? Let me go!"

John was fighting to hold her and get the bag open at the same time. Children in the train were gawking in astonishment. Pokey batted the air with a hand as if to signal, *Stay there!* and cried, "Wait, John. Please!"

He paused. "Huh? What's wrong?"

Miss Vanderpugh's hair was all straggly, her face was red. Pokey said, "Let her go."

"But, Pokey—"

Pokey hoped she wasn't wrong. Miss Vanderpugh was a CCer, however lowly. "Don't worry. Miss V.—"

The woman shook away from John's grasp. She was grinning at Pokey. "You really are alive."

"Yes."

"And you've stopped the train. Knocked Matron Shrank down. How could you?"

"*We* could," Pokey said bravely. "Now, you have one chance. Will you watch the children for us?"

Behind her, Hannah whispered in Pokey's ear. "And keep them quiet."

"And keep them quiet."

Miss Vanderpugh put her hands to her hair, jabbing at it. She was crying. "Yes. Oh, thank you, oh, bless you all, I'll do whatever you say." She turned and fled back onto the train, leaving John flabbergasted.

"Excellent," said Hannah. Pokey saw with surprise that she was wearing Matron's coat and silly red hat (the hat squashed a little and perched haphazardly on her head). She looked at Ross. "Turn on headquarters again."

The man sounded alarmed. "Calling Harpers Ferry. Clinton . . . Skip Clinton, are you there?" He spoke to someone else. "You see? They don't answer. I've been calling and calling. Clinton's always around when a train comes through. Do you think there's a problem?"

A second man said, "Keep trying. There may be. We might have to call Brunswick. Or go see."

The first tried again. "Clinton . . . Skip Clinton. Do you hear me? Hello."

Hannah ordered, "Ross, turn on the mike."

Ross flipped the switch, then held up his thumb. Hannah rubbed her hands in concentration. Then she squashed Matron's hat more securely, took a breath . . . and stepped into the inner circle.

"Hello?" She squinted up at the camera. "You calling Mr. Clinton?

There was a strangled gasp at headquarters. "Hello? Who are you?"

"Miss Hannah Lucas. You wanting Mr. Clinton?"

"Y-yes. Where is he?"

"He can't come to the station just now. He's busy."

"Busy? Doing what?"

Hannah looked off toward her mountain for half a second, drew the lapels of Matron's coat together, and gazed back up at the camera. "The hydroelectric. Twigs and logs were clogging up the intake bays. Almost shut off one generator. We're fixing it."

"What? The plant? It's going down?"

"No. We're fixing it," Hannah repeated firmly.

"You?"

"Yes. I help. We all help when we need to. You want me to fetch Mr. Clinton? I . . . I guess he could get away."

"No! No, you tell him to keep on. Just report when he's done."

"Yessir. It may take a while. I'll come back and let you know."

"OK. Who . . . who did you say you are?" The electronic files had started clicking.

Hannah winced and frowned. "Miss Hannah Lucas," she said, scowling at the deep eye.

"Lucas, Lucas." *Click* came the sound of a photograph being taken. "Ah, good. Now we've got you."

"You all through?"

"Almost. Did you . . . pass under the camera earlier? Looked like someone else . . . ah, from above. Guess I was seeing things. Didn't think there were two hats like that in the world."

Hannah put her hand to her head and smiled coyly. "You like my hat? I've had it for years. Yes, I walked here. I'm making tea for them that's working. That all right?"

"Yes, yes. Of course. The train get through?"

Hannah looked right at the gleaming middle car. "It's gone."

"OK. Thank you, Miss Lucas. Over and out."

Hannah stepped across the circle to John. Ross flipped the microphone off. He laughed, leaning far out the window to shout, "Hooray!"

The sisters were lugging Matron out of sight. Pokey clapped her hands. "He believed you, Hannah."

"And why wouldn't he, I'd like to know?" she inquired with a dignified air. "Now. Let's get finished here. You should be going." She and John headed around the building.

Ross ran down to the parking lot. "Congratulations, all of you," he exclaimed, clapping Hannah on the back five or six times.

When Matron Shrank was loaded (cozy and silent in her burlap bag), John said, "We'll come with you," and the procession set off with Maude and Sissy leading the way, John pushing the garden cart, Hannah steadying the load by holding one of Matron's serviceable black oxfords, and Pokey and Ross coming along behind.

At the fort, they put Matron in one room with Tom and the engineer, Helene and Skip in the other, dividing CCers and sexes as best they could. John barred the doors, checking them twice.

"I'll take the first watch," Hannah announced. She went around the corner and brought out her rocker, which she placed in front of the two arched doors. (*That's what she went back for,* Pokey thought. *Of course.*) The chair looked different on the sunny grass, bigger somehow.

No one moved. The six of them were caught for a moment, speechless.

The raid was over. A complete success. The train had been stopped; it wouldn't leave unless one of them drove it. But it was full of children who would soon be needing things: to go to the bathroom, get a drink, have a hurt fixed, find a place to sleep and something to eat. As they wakened from the lulling of the litany they would need even more.

As for the opposition, they were knocked out, tied up, bound and locked in the red brick building. They couldn't be left like that forever. Soon they would require attention, too.

And nothing else was changed, anywhere in the world.

Pokey had an awful, letdown sense of, *We won. So what? Now what?*

Hannah must have been thinking the same thing, for she said, "So, John. I see what you mean. About leaving."

"Yes. Well, we've made a beginning. I don't know how far we'll get before we run into trouble. People might see us going back. In Brunswick, even. We'll get to the city today—somehow. You . . . better be prepared for investigators out here. I'll get word to you, and send help if I can."

"We'll be all right," said Hannah.

"Ross left four cars behind your house, with keys in them and full of gas. In case you need to go somewhere or move the prisoners. Hannah doesn't drive, but—"

"We do," Maude announced, and Sissy nodded. Both looked so confident that Pokey thought, *They really could be all right, the three of them.*

Hannah said, "We're going to block the track, with trees or that baggage cart or something. So no train will get by. Excepting one you drive, of course."

John nodded, smiling. "You're always ahead of me."

"We have to go," Ross said. "Ready?"

"Yes." John didn't look at Pokey when he asked, "You?"

She couldn't speak; she shook her head.

John and Ross kissed the three women.

"Good luck," said Maude.

"Be careful." Sissy sniffed.

"Please come back," Hannah whispered.

Ross brushed Pokey's arm as if he couldn't say goodbye, John hugged her briefly, and they strode away.

Hannah was sitting in the rocker, her stout stick beside her. Pokey threw herself down, buried her head in the old woman's lap. "No, no," she cried. "Don't let them go."

Bending over, Hannah touched her shoulders. "You have to decide. Now is the time."

"I . . ."

"Whatever you do, whichever you choose . . ." Her voice broke. "I love you, just the same."

Pokey squeezed Hannah's skirt. She could see herself

in a few minutes, standing by the tracks, hearing the last sounds of the train, desperate to know where it was.

I'm so far out of line, so far from being one of those kids anymore . . . even if I was caught, captured, and put somewhere, I'd be . . . me, like I am now . . .

Even drugged? No. But . . .

The children, the bland announcer at headquarters, other CCers she'd never seen: she wanted to know what was happening to them. Experience their surprise. Help decide what to do.

Maybe safety wasn't all-important anymore.

"Hannah," she said, "I think I have to go."

"I was afraid so."

"Do you understand?"

"Yes. Just come back."

They embraced, then Hannah urged hoarsely, "You'd better hurry. It's a long walk if you miss the train."

Pokey wiped her eyes, grinned at the Watson sisters. "I'll flip the switch for you," Sissy promised. "I remember."

Pokey started running. "Hey, you guys," she hollered. "Wait for me! Wait up. I'm coming too!"